THE LONELIEST ROBOT

By Andrew Glennon

Illustrated by Matt Dixon

The Loneliest Robot.

Written by Andrew Glennon.
Illustrations by Matt Dixon.
© 2017 Andrew Glennon. All Rights Reserved.
First Edition.
First Published 2017.

Edited by KT Editing Services
(www.ktediting.com)
Illustration Credit (Lifelike drawing in Chapter 30) and thanks to
Paul Cadden
(www.paulcadden.com)

ISBN 13: 978-1530876587
ISBN 10: 1530876583

Visit the author's website at
www.theloneliestrobot.com

Visit the illustrators website at
www.mattdixon.co.uk

This book is dedicated to my mother, Alice Glennon
(1938-2014)

Selected Quotations

"Aspire not to have more, but to BE more."
Oscar Romero

"When I was five years old, my mother always told me that
happiness was the key to life.
When I went to school, they asked me what I wanted to be when I
grew up. I wrote down 'happy'.
They told me I didn't understand the assignment, and I told them
they didn't understand life."
John Lennon

"Non-stop pursuing of wealth will only turn a person into a twisted
being, just like me.
Material things lost can be found. But there is one thing that can
never be found when it is lost – Life.
Whichever stage in life we are at right now, with time, we will face
the day when the curtain comes down.
Treasure love for your family, love for your spouse,
love for your friends.
Treat yourself well. Cherish others."
Steve Jobs (extract from his final words)
Co-Founder and CEO of Apple Computers

Prologue: First Light

Sixty years ago

(In a South-East China fishing village)

The young girl sat by the old harbour, watching all the local fishermen push away in their small boats, all of them hoping for fair weather and a good catch. It was first light, and a new day was just beginning when she noticed a father and son walking down the hill and along the beach, fishing nets draped around their shoulders. The young boy smiled and waved to the young girl. Every morning, the young girl returned a hopeful smile and an eager wave.

The father and son dragged a small fishing boat from the dry, morning sands and pushed it out into the shallow waves. Then they jumped aboard, both glowing in excited anticipation of a new day. *They seem like two happy souls*, the girl thought. She watched as they drifted away from land and glided out to meet the early morning horizon. She stared at the silhouetted image of a father and son, happily fishing together under a dark, forbidding sky.

Distant thunder rumbled out at sea as a biting wind immersed the harbour. The young girl knew a storm was coming.

THE LONELIEST ROBOT
Part 1

1
The Delivery

Robert Karma was a normal twelve-year-old boy. He lived in a normal house, in a normal town, in a normal country. Sadly, his parents were very normal as well, and they were *always* incredibly busy. Actually, they weren't just busy – they were too busy *being* busy to do anything else. Robert did not have any brothers or sisters, and he didn't have many friends either. Quite often, he felt lonely.

Robert's dad, Keith Karma, worked away from home most of the time. His dad travelled the world to help a big, rich company become even richer. The company paid his dad a lot of money, and this made him feel vital and successful. Sometimes his dad would Skype home from some hotel from around the world (the calls were always the same predictable conversations but never felt comfortable or real to Robert). Robert had much preferred it when his dad was at home so he could listen to a real bedtime story while sitting right next to each other. He liked to fall asleep cuddled up right up next to him, able to smell his father's familiar aftershave. They hadn't shared a bedtime story for almost five years now, and Robert missed the time they shared together. His dad was away so much, he was starting to feel like a stranger to Robert.

When his dad returned home from his work trips, he would either be camped in his office (in the converted office loft), babbling on some telephone conference, or going shopping with his mum.

"No point in working so hard if we can't enjoy it all!" Robert's dad would always say.

His parents frequently went out to buy more stuff. It was always bigger stuff than the stuff they already had. A bigger car, a bigger TV set, a bigger fridge to store the bigger food, even bigger pillows so they could sit up in the big bed while using their bigger mobile devices. Just a few years ago, they had needed to buy a bigger house to keep all the bigger stuff. Robert's dad was always using his mobile phone – he was so fast at typing on it that his thumbs had developed muscles. He was a very busy man.

"Look, Robert! 1,434 emails, all received in just the last three hours. Everyone needs *me*. I must get working on them right now!"

Robert's dad would then disappear for hours – or sometimes days – to do more work and to take more calls.

Robert's mum was very lazy, and she would spend her days in bed watching the shopping channel or hypnotised by placing orders on her laptop, buying more and more stuff from the internet. Every day, parcels would get delivered to the house with stuff that Mum thought she absolutely needed. Whatever his parents did and whatever they bought, they were always too distracted or tired to do anything with Robert. They told him they needed to watch TV and drink wine to relax, which they did every single night, both happily ignoring each other and shaking their heads at the screen.

One day, Robert's dad looked up from his mobile device. "You know what, Robert? I thought it was time we found you a friend! You keep getting in our way and interrupting my work calls. I think a new friend for you would make life so much easier for us. I was in China on business just last week and came across something in Tangbian Bay, just off the South China Sea.

"Some factory or other had just closed down, and there were hundreds of redundant robots for sale in a local market. I managed to get one that looked a bit different, and it seemed quite friendly enough. It seemed to take a liking to my irresistible charm, as it followed me for over two hours! Persistent little fellow. Your mother will love him, and all her friends will be just green with envy when she tells them we have a house robot! I just received a text from the supplier to inform me that it should get delivered around—" *Dingdong!* the doorbell chimed "—now!"

Robert raced to the door and opened it to see a large wooden shipping crate being lifted by two deliverymen from the back of a truck. They brought the crate into the house and placed it in the hallway. The package was a large wooden shipping crate with large red words stamped on each side of the container: FRAGILE SEA FREIGHT. HANDLE WITH CARE. YAMANUCHI ROBOTICS. There were also some red Chinese writing symbols stamped on the crate, which Robert didn't understand.

您是人类的一种生活活出它。 电池不需要!

The deliverymen left the crate in the hallway, and after getting a delivery signature from Robert's dad, they drove away in their truck. Mr Karma took one look at the crate and, realising some manual effort would be required to open it, backed away, muttering, "Well, it's all yours, son! I have a conference call with Uganda right now, and Mum's busy ordering bigger and better spoons. I'll leave it with you to sort it out! Have fun and remember, the gift is yours, and it's your responsibility to take care of it."

Robert was really puzzled now, "What does all that red Chinese writing mean Dad? Is it a dangerous package? It could be important."

Immediately, Roberts father selected an application on his mobile device and quickly pointed the device at the red Chinese writing that was stamped across the wooden crate. The device flashed and after two seconds made a beep that made Mr Karma smile.

"Clever little app this one Robert. Point and translate. Ideal for understanding foreign restaurant menus! Works in 130 languages. Anyway…this Chinese translation doesn't make much sense at all… You are Human. One Life. Live It. No Batteries Required."

Before Robert could answer, his father was already trotting up the stairs while shouting through his headset, "Hello? Hello? Can you hear me, Uganda? Is anyone else on the conference line yet?" He then disappeared from view as he reached the top of the stairs.

Robert Karma stood alone in the shadow of the giant large shipping crate positioned before him. He started to wonder how on earth he was going to open it. He stopped wondering when the box made a deep rumbling noise and began to shake.

2
The Mystery Cleaner

The shipping crate rumbled and rocked slowly. It did this for several minutes, squeaking and creaking, and just as Robert was about to run and tell his parents, the side of the shipping crate that was facing him fell to the floor with a deep thud. A large mass of packing straw spewed out from the shipping container and covered Robert's feet, knees, waist, and shoulders. With just his head sticking out above the packing straw, he peered into the shipping crate as the air filled with bits of straw and dust. All he could see was more shipping straw, densely packed inside the dark container.

He moved very slowly and leant closer into the silent crate. The packaging straw was everywhere, and as he edged closer into the box, a stray strand of straw somehow poked itself up into one of his nostrils. Immediately, he reacted with a powerful and loud sneeze. "Aaaahhhhhhhhtchoooooo!"

When he opened his eyes after his mega-sneeze, a clean, pristine white handkerchief had appeared in front of his face. It was held by what looked like small metal fingers. Intuitively, Robert accepted the handkerchief, and as he wiped his nose with his eyes and mouth both wide open, the metallic hand slowly disappeared back down into the shipping straw that swamped Robert – and its mystery handkerchief provider.

"Thank you," Robert whispered as he gazed into the packaging straw. There was no answer. Robert started to feel a little awkward, and he backed away from the shipping crate and whatever lay beneath the sprawl of straw that almost filled the entire hallway in his home. He retreated up the stairs and sat on the middle step as he locked his gaze on the crate. He sat there, fixated and fascinated, waiting for something to happen. He must have sat in silent observation for at least fifteen minutes before the silence was broken by the sound of the doorbell. He felt locked in place, however, and stayed sitting while the doorbell rang out several more times.

"Will someone just answer that door?" wailed Robert's mother, Consooma Karma, from the other room. "Can't you see I am very busy watching the shopping channel in the lounge and ordering more stuff on the Internet? My God, do I have to do *everything* around here?"

The doorbell rang again as Mrs Karma wobbled from the lounge room and into the hallway, which was now entirely littered with the open shipping crate and spilled packing straw. She stood still in her tracks as the doorbell rang one last time.

"And what the hell is this?" she screamed as she locked her bright green eyes on to Robert. "This place really does look like a pigsty now! What the hell are you playing at, Robert Karma? Can't you see I am busy? My God!" She kept muttering angrily as she opened the door to accept yet another delivery – this time she had ordered a spare TV set, for the extra TV set that they kept in the spare room. All in all, they now had twelve TV sets in the house. That was four sets per person. How many TVs could someone watch at once?

"You, boy!" she shrieked as she closed the front door. She turned to Robert, who was still sitting on the stairs, and pointed her long fat finger at her nervous-looking son.

"You are such a disappointment to me! Just look at you, sitting there like a *little lost soul*. All I want is some peace and quiet and just look at this place! Clean this up right now. If it's not done in ten minutes then you, boy, are in serious jelly! Why can't you be like the perfect, beautiful children I see on all of those brilliant TV adverts?"

As Mrs Karma continued to shout and rant, Robert noticed a yellow glow emitting from within the shipping crate. He found the gentle light glow enticing and strangely soothing.

"Are you listening to me? Ten minutes, that's all. You got that?"

Mrs Karma slammed the lounge door behind her before Robert had the chance to answer her, or to tell her about the mysterious glowing package in the hallway. As usual, she was too busy to notice anything. Robert did understand one thing, though, and that was that his mother was an angry and selfish person who only cared about herself and acquiring more stuff to try to make her feel happier. If he did not clean the mess up in the hallway within the ten-minute deadline, then his mother would not hesitate in dreaming up some nasty punishment for him.

He stood and made his way to the cupboard under the stairs, where he would find the vacuum cleaner and other cleaning products to tidy the hallway mess before his mother got even madder. As he opened the cupboard and leant inside to reach for the vacuum cleaner, he heard some muffled noises behind him. He turned to see that the front door was now open and that the large shipping crate had disappeared.

He went to the front door and walked down the garden path, looking to see any sign of the large wooden box. He couldn't see anything as he looked up and down his street, and he noted that it was just another ordinary day. Feeling puzzled and a little deflated, he started to move back up the garden path that led to the front door and as he walked, he thought he heard the familiar sound of a vacuum cleaner. As he reached the entrance to his house, the sound suddenly stopped. He stepped into his hallway again, and what *had* been a complete mess that consisted of splintered wood and packing straw was now a pristine and spotlessly clean and empty hallway. There was no sign of anything.

Robert stood there, perplexed and confused. He had only turned his back for a few seconds, and the mess had entirely disappeared. He thought back to when he'd heard the sound of the vacuum cleaner as he stood outside the house. Just as he moved towards the cleaning cupboard under the staircase, his mother returned to the hallway. She positioned her bulk between Robert and the cleaning closet.

"Well, well, boy, not bad at all, and all in two minutes. Next time I won't be as generous as ten minutes! Now go to your room and sort that tip out as well!"

"But Mum," Robert replied, "I didn't clean this mess up!"

His mother cackled and looked as if she had just drunk some sour vinegar. "Well, it certainly wasn't your father, and as the lady of the house, you know I'm far too important to do any cleaning."

She continued to moan, but once again, Robert's attention drifted towards the cleaning cupboard behind where his mother now stood. A gentle yellow glow pulsed through the horizontal slats of the cabinet door.

Mrs Karma continued to pontificate and finished with, "And of course, Robert, it's all your fault! Now leave me in peace, I need to order some new toothpaste tube dispensers with Wi-Fi connectivity – 'essential for the modern home', the advert said. Go to your bedroom now!"

"But Mum—" Robert said pleadingly.

"Bed now!" she barked back.

Robert skulked slowly up the stairs and offered no further resistance to his mother. The formidable-looking woman stood at the bottom of the stairs with her arms folded tight and shoulders hunched, as if she were freezing. As he ascended the stairs, Robert peeked through the bannister and could still see a gentle yellow glow shine through the cleaning cupboard door slats on to the hallway floor, which was now spotlessly clean and gleaming.

3
Night-time in the Garden Shed

Robert lay in bed, gazing at his bedroom ceiling. He had gone to bed earlier with a strange feeling inside him – it was a little bit like how he felt on Christmas Eve when he was younger. He felt a nervous excitement that was stopping him falling into a deep sleep, but this time he was not excited about Santa Claus or trying to hear sleigh bells during the night. Instead, he was intrigued by what had happened earlier with the shipping container and the disappearing cleaner-upper. What on earth was hiding in the cleaning cupboard under the stairs? He lay in the dark, trying hard to hear any noises coming from downstairs, but all he could hear was the distant drone of his father's regular – and very annoying – snoring rumbling from his parents' bedroom.

Robert glanced at his bedside radio clock. The red digits glowed 02:58 a.m., and he knew he wouldn't be able to sleep. His mind was just too curious. Just as the clock reached 03:12 a.m., he heard a noise, which sounded like it had come from downstairs. His heart started to thud in his chest, and he felt frozen to his bed in fear. It went quiet for a few minutes, and he started to think he must have imagined the noise when he then heard another sound coming from downstairs, this time like a door creaking open. Robert thought about shouting out for his parents and telling them about the noises but quickly dismissed the idea once he suspected his parents would either ignore him or yell at him to go back to sleep. He decided there and then that he was going to investigate the noises and quietly slipped out of his bed and tip-toed over to his bedroom door, trying very carefully not to make any noises as he moved across the room. Slowly and silently, he opened his bedroom door and crept to the top of the stairs, gazing down into the total darkness of his home. He was just about to take his first step down the stairs when a familiar shout made his body jolt.

"You're snoring like a pig again, Keith Karma! Just shut your cakehole and let me get some kip!" It was his mother complaining to his father, and while it wasn't unusual (she always complained about something), it did surprise Robert as he stood still in the mysterious darkness.

He felt cold and could sense a gentle fresh air flowing through the house as he started to move down the stairs. His vision was adjusting to the darkness now, and as he reached the bottom of the stairs, he turned and could see that the cleaning cupboard door was wide open. He reached out to switch on the hallway light, and as he did so, he once again felt a breeze of fresh air against his face. Without turning the light on, he leant forward and peered into the kitchen. He could see a bright full moon reflecting down on the kitchen floor tiles, and he realised that the moon was shining through the kitchen's back door, which was standing wide open into the night. He moved towards the open door and could now understand why the house was filled with a gentle air – it was blowing in from the chilly night.

Robert reached the back doorway and stood to look out into the garden. He could not see anything unusual and could only hear the familiar quiet drip of the kitchen tap as he scanned the garden for any signs of movement. It was still a few hours away from the early morning birdsong that would usually fill the garden.

He stood there in his red pyjamas and bare feet, and even though he could feel a slight chill from the night-time air, he stepped out into the garden, the cold patio stones under his feet as he walked towards the lawn area. Soon, he could feel the wet dewy grass between his toes as he stood on the lawn under the quiet moonlight. He must have stood there for a few minutes before he realised that the bottom of his pyjamas were already soaking wet.

Suddenly, he heard a sound. It sounded like cans or boxes falling over, and it came from the bottom of the garden. Robert thought it could be a cat or a dog moving around in the night and he was about to retreat to the safety of his home when he noticed the gentle yellow glow. It was coming from the old and tatty garden shed, and he noticed the yellow light now filled the shed's side window.

He didn't fully understand why he did what he did next. Rather than return to the safety of his house, he felt compelled to go to the shed to investigate further. He didn't care that it was cold or that his pyjamas were getting even wetter as he moved slowly across the grass. As he approached, he noticed that the shed door was only slightly open and he heard more sounds, as if stuff was getting moved around inside. Only then did it occur to Robert that burglars could be inside the shed, and he could be about to disturb a crime!

He heard a distant dog bark, and he pondered returning to the security of his house. Then, once again, he noticed the gentle yellow light glowing from the shed window frame. The various garden tools and equipment that stood in the shed were silhouetted against the soft yellow light. *Maybe the burglars had a yellow beam torch*, Robert thought as he moved closer to the shed door. The sounds suddenly stopped once he pushed open the door with a creak. He was very scared now and could hear his heart thumping in his chest as he moved his head inside the shed to take a closer look. What he saw amazed him.

The inside of the garden shed was usually a complete mess. It contained several old garden tools such broken lawnmowers, shovels, wheelbarrows, hedge trimmers, hammers, garden hoses, watering cans, etc. Like a mini scrapyard, the equipment would be discarded and piled up to collect dust. However, Robert was now amazed that all the stuff in the shed now looked spotlessly clean, with everything stored in the tidiest order. He had never seen the shed look (and smell) so clean before.

On one side of the shed, all the tools were hanging from a hook on the wall or stacked very neatly. Robert recognised an old garden hose reel and an old tin watering can, but he did not recognise what was behind the hanging hose reel and old tin watering can. In the darkness of the shed, he saw something that had a dark copper metal base, with a round dark window in the centre. *Maybe it was a broken old washing machine*, thought Robert, as he quietly whispered the three large letters printed on the metal base, just above the round glass window: UMA.

Just as Robert whispered these letters, a very faint red light started to glow from the inside of the round glass window. He stepped closer and reached out to place his hand towards the light, which seemed to glow more brightly as his hand touched the cool surface of the glass panel. Robert smiled in the red glow and somehow, at that moment, he felt warm and calm. It was only once he removed his hand, and as the red glow faded, that the familiar yellow light came shining from behind some old tools that were hanging in the shed. He stepped away, and as he did so, a small robot stepped forward from behind the shed clutter. The robot was smaller than Robert and now stood still, staring at him. He had the old watering can in his hand, and Robert figured out that the robot had just been using it to water the potted plant that stood beside him.

Robert noticed that the yellow lights sat inside a round dark metal head, and they were not torchlights but the robot's eyes. The robot stood silently and quietly inspected Robert, its yellow eyes gently pulsing as it observed the bewildered boy. In turn, Robert looked back at the robot, which was about the height of his shoulder. He noticed that the robot's head had no mouth or ears and simply just housed two large yellow eyes.

Strangely, Robert felt no sense of fear. Instead, he felt an instant connection with the robot. He reached out his hand as he said, "Hello, I am Robert Karma. Welcome to my home."

The robot stood silent and motionless for a few minutes while Robert stood with his hand outstretched. He was just about to withdraw his reach when the robot lifted his hand out and both boy and robot made a long and gentle handshake. Robert noticed a soft red light glow in the robot's chest window as he said to the robot, "My, my. You do look like a lost soul! Let's get back to the house before we catch our death of cold!"

The robot did not respond, and it just continued to stare at the boy while its red light quietly pulsed a throbbing glow under the letters UMA. Its head slowly moved up and down as it studied Robert, each small motion making a quiet whirring but relaxing sound.

"C'mon . . . it's freezing out here!" said Robert, as again he eyed the three letters on the chest of the robot. "So, I guess I call you UMA?" he asked as he reached for the robot's hand and pulled him towards the house.

The little robot seemed more than happy to follow him.

4
The Breakfast Order

Robert Karma awoke but his eyes remained closed, his body still enjoying the deep, warm comfort of sleep. Huddled in his bed, he could hear the usual morning noises coming from around his house. Birds were chirping happily from a neighbour's garden, and his mother was watching the shopping channel on her bedroom TV. In the loft above, his father was yapping away on a conference call with other work colleagues based around the world.

There was a strange sound of squeaking coming from nearby. It stopped but started again, and it came from the direction of Robert's bedroom window. He opened one eye and peeked a look at the window, which was just a few feet from where he lay in his bed. The squeaking continued, and Robert noticed something moving behind one of the dark blue curtains. He wasn't puzzled for too long, as he soon realised what was behind the curtain once he looked down at the gap between the bottom of the curtains and the carpeted bedroom floor. In the gap, he could see two metallic feet standing on tiptoes, moving side to side as the window squeaking continued.

Robert smiled to himself as he remembered what had happened during the early hours of that day, and how he had discovered the little robot in the garden shed at 4 a.m. He recalled how the robot had gladly followed him back to his bedroom, and how smoothly and silently the robot could walk. Climbing the stairs in the darkness presented no problem for it, and it had moved very quietly so Robert's parents had not been disturbed from sleep.

Robert leant out from the bed and reached across to pull the curtain aside, revealing the little robot was now very busy cleaning his bedroom window with one of his socks. The robot seemed highly focused on the task as it reached to the top of the window to clean all areas of the glass.

"Good morning, erm, UMA. What you doing?" asked Robert.

The robot stopped performing his cleaning task, turning its metal head to face Robert. Its eyes pulsed a gentle yellow glow again.

"You *can* hear me, can't you?" Robert continued, not sure if the robot could understand, as it had no obvious ears on its head. The robot slowly nodded, its neck making a purring whirring noise as its head moved up and down.

"But where are your ears?" Robert inquired as he sat up on the edge of his bed.

The robot stepped away from the curtain and handed Robert the sock it had been using for cleaning the window. The robot stood before Robert, and they faced each other at an equal level. It then stepped closer to Robert and smoothly turned around, so it was now facing away from him. With its back now facing Robert, the robot raised one hand and pointed a metal finger to the back of its metal head. Robert followed the robot's direction and noticed a small, square, speaker-type grill, similar to that of a small radio, which was fastened to the lower part of the robot's head.

"Ahhh, so this is how you hear? This is your ear?"

Without turning around, the robot nodded its head slowly to confirm Robert's observation was correct. Robert also noticed some writing that was stencilled just below the speaker grill. The writing was minuscule, and he moved closer to read the words aloud.

"Yamanuchi Robotics. Universal Metamorphic Android – Batteries not required/Model number 001 of 002."

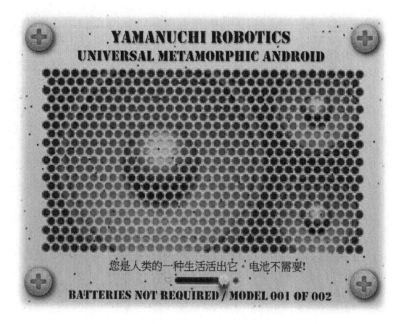

He also noticed some Chinese writing that he didn't understand and realised that this robot was model one of a set of two. The robot stepped away and turned to face Robert again.

"No batteries? But how? Don't you need to recharge every night? I mean, how do you keep going? What keeps you going?"

The robot turned to face Robert again and extended its hands, taking hold of Robert's hands and gently pulling him up from where he was sitting on the bed. Robert looked down at his smaller companion as they both stood there holding hands, and just as Robert starting feeling a bit weird about standing in his bedroom holding hands with a robot, UMA moved Robert's hands towards the circular light panel on the robot's chest. His open hands were gently placed on the surface of the circle panel as it started to emit a vague red glow. Amazingly, the red light also gave out a warm, gentle heat.

"You get your power from this?" Robert asked as his open hands rested over the glowing robot chest. UMA nodded as the red light quietly purred.

The moment was quickly interrupted as the bedroom door flung open. It was Robert's father, Mr Keith Karma, who never knocked on the door before entering. Keith Karma was a large fat man with a rounded face and a rather pig-like snout for a nose that sat below thick, round-framed spectacles. He had a shiny bald head but did have some hair in the form of a big thick black moustache that resembled an unmade bed.

He was loud, rude, and always in a hurry to do something else – so much so that he found it difficult to concentrate on anything for more than eight seconds before something else distracted him (usually a new text or email). Robert's father was very proud to hold the record for sending and receiving the record amount of emails in his company. The email count totalled 2.3 million, but this number increased every day as he continued to be hypnotised by his mobile device. He even had a backup device to use whenever his other device was charging.

Keith Karma entered the bedroom without looking up from his mobile device, on which he was busy using two enormous thumbs to type a message to a work colleague in Tanzania. Robert had noticed that his father's thumbs had grown twice as big in the last three years, and he concluded that they had developed super thumb muscles from the constant exercise from using mobile devices so much.

Robert's father spoke as he continued typing on his device. "Your mother has been shouting for you, Robert! She must have shouted for you at least once this morning. She is famished and wants her morning latte, dusted with caramel chocolate, and a Swiss croissant filled with toasted marshmallow. Now if you're not too busy, as I obviously am, could you please attend to her now?"

Mr Karma turned without looking up from his device and walked out of the bedroom, but continued with his breakfast order.

"I'll take some French toast, chocolate porridge, cream donuts, and I'll try some of that new yoghurt stuff to stay healthy and keep the weight down. Bring it up to my office – I have a global conference call now with 182 people. Should be an exciting call. It's the monthly metrics review call!"

With that, his father shuffled off and bounced upstairs to his office. Robert and UMA stood motionless as they heard his father dial into the conference call while shouting loudly to introduce himself to his 182 colleagues.

"That was my dad. He's always very busy and says he is critical to the success of his company. Not sure if he even noticed you, he doesn't notice me most of the time around here." Robert spoke in a quiet and almost apologetic voice. UMA nodded slowly.

Robert continued, "I guess I better get breakfast moving before I get ready for school. If I don't, Mum will go crazy if she has to get out of bed to shout at me."

Robert quickly dashed into the bathroom to wash and returned to his bedroom to change into his school uniform. While he filled his school bag with his incomplete homework, he could smell an inviting aroma of freshly baked breakfast coming from the kitchen below. His mouth dropped open as he raced downstairs and into the kitchen to investigate the source of the delicious smell.

Sitting on the kitchen top were two trays – each one contained breakfast for Robert's parents. The coffee smelled and looked delicious and had that beautiful artistic frothy dusted chocolate topping that you only get at real and very expensive coffee shops. Even better, each tray included wonderful fresh pastries that looked like an expert French patisserie had baked them that very morning.

All of the items that Robert's father had ordered were laid out and perfectly presented on the serving trays, and each tray held a delightful red carnation in a small and elegant glass vase. Robert couldn't believe how the little robot had managed all this. It all looked so professional and   appetising. After a few moments of admiring the breakfast, Robert looked up to see UMA standing at the kitchen sink, now busy cleaning the items he had used to create such a fantastic-looking meal.

Just then, a familiar banging thud came from the kitchen ceiling. It was Robert's mother banging her heavy, flabby foot on her bedroom floor to remind him she was hungry for breakfast.

"Wow, UMA! I had better get this upstairs. I'll ask you how you did all this later. But it sure looks great!"

Robert went upstairs, carefully balancing the breakfast tray that was destined for his mother. UMA stood silently at the kitchen sink while he finished the dish-washing. He looked out from the kitchen window behind the sink and noticed that it was a bright and beautiful morning. A flock of snow geese flew in the cloudless blue sky, escaping to another country on their annual migration, while a cheerful robin sat on the top of the garden fence and chirped to welcome a new day.

UMA did not feel any need to escape from his new home, as somehow he felt he belonged with Robert. His chest light gave a fuzzy red glow and produced a blush of warmth from the kitchen window, as red as the breast of the robin that happily sang to him from the garden fence.

5
UMA Satsuma Surprise

That day, Robert went to school as normal, but all he could think about was his new and very helpful robot friend, UMA. His parents were most impressed with the breakfasts that Robert had served them earlier that morning and had even almost thanked him.

His mother, Consooma Karma, had been busy ordering stuff on her laptop while sprawled in her colossal bed. She had looked up and almost smiled at Robert once she smelled the fresh coffee and pastries drifting up from her breakfast tray, but this quickly disappeared when her laptop beeped loudly to notify her that her order (for electrically heated slippers) would not get delivered until the next day.

His father had almost looked up from his mobile phone as he snatched and noisily gobbled at his breakfast. His dad did manage to mumble a "Wow, great job!" as Robert walked out of the office. Sadly, the compliment was not meant for Robert – he soon realised that his father was talking to another person on the telephone conference call.

His father continued shouting into his phone headset. "Great, great job, Pedro, you absolutely smashed the monthly sales target in Venezuela! We are killing the competition! Awesome! Now let's see how Bermuda are doing. Is Winston on the call?"

Robert didn't mind school. It was better than being stuck at home with his parents, and at least he got to talk and play with other people. He especially liked music and art lessons, as he was sometimes encouraged to create something new and unique, but lately, even those experiences had become quite dull. Music was all about learning how to read music and practice repetitive musical scales, and his art lessons were currently about how to calculate mathematical angles to ensure "drawing perspective" was accurate. It didn't feel very natural. Robert much preferred it when he was allowed to do stuff without having to follow the rules. It was like he was being trained to do these things just like everyone else. Everyone in the class was learning the same thing, so Robert thought everyone would end up creating the same thing. Now, where was the fun in that?

That day, Robert couldn't wait for school to end so that he could get back home to see UMA. Earlier, before he had left the house for school, he had put UMA in the garden shed to keep him away from his parents, and the little robot seemed happy enough to continue tidying up all the junk in the shed. Robert hoped UMA would stay quietly occupied in the shed and patiently wait for him to return from school. However, things sometimes don't quite work out as planned.

Robert ran home from school – it was just a five-minute uphill run to his home – and raced straight to the back garden gate. He was most surprised by the sight that greeted him as he opened the gate. The garden looked amazing and was now transformed into something quite beautiful.

When he had left for school, the garden had been as plain and predictable as every other garden in the street. It had featured a boring square garden lawn and a few green bushes lined up against the surrounding garden fence. That was obviously before UMA had got to work, as it was now a mini oasis in the middle of a suburban street.

The lawn was now a spiral-patterned swirl of lush grass, with red and white flowers fluttering at the edges of the garden. Robert could smell the overwhelming scent of summer roses and stood to stare, now transfixed by the bright, vivid colours of the flowers. He then noticed that the garden bushes were skilfully trimmed and sculpted to resemble delightful shapes and figures. One bush was now shaped like a majestic flying angel, and one of the older tatty bushes was transformed to look like a flying eagle. The wooden garden fence was painted with hundreds of dazzling leaves, each one a different shape and colour, to form a wondrous mosaic.

Robert stood still, rooted to the spot, while absorbing the view in front of him. He looked at the end of the garden and there, standing in the doorway of the shed, was UMA. He had an old tin watering can rocking in his hand and further welcomed Robert into the garden by raising his hand and gently waving at his friend. Robert raced over and was about to enquire how he had transformed the garden when he heard the familiar high-pitched shrill of his mother's voice coming from the garden patio area.

"Service please, house slave!" she shouted as she lay on a sun lounger. Although Robert's mother was very fat, this did not stop her from sunbathing in a tiny bikini while proudly wearing her expensive designer sunglasses. Robert noticed how her marble-like white belly flesh wobbled as she shrieked, "My glass is running dry, robot man! I need another of your cocktail creations!"

She followed this order with the most annoying laugh you could imagine. It started as a cheap snigger, before slowly building up to a crackling whooping laugh that made her massive thighs shake like giant water balloons.

"I'll try another robot special. What did I call it? The UMA Satsuma Surprise?"

Robert stood amazed as UMA sprang into action. He turned and entered the garden shed, and Robert followed him as he reached a small table that was filled with various glasses and bottles. Quickly, UMA took an old paint pot and filled it with different items – an old leaf, some dried stale orange peel, fly spray, WD40, a pinch of garden fertiliser, and finally adding a sprinkle of dirty water from the old tin watering can that UMA held in his hand. He then added some ice he had stored in a wheelbarrow, placed a lid on the old paint pot, and proceeded to shake it as he turned to face Robert.

"UMA! You're not going to give her that, are you? It looks rank awful. It will make her sick!" Robert whispered.

UMA carried on shaking the cocktail in the paint pot and then poured it into a cocktail glass.

"Seriously, UMA, that stuff stinks as well!"

The little robot slowly placed the paint pot on to the floor of the shed and removed the lid before gently putting one metallic finger on to Robert's mouth as if to shush him. He slowly poured the dirty liquid into a cocktail glass, and Robert watched in awe as the robot then raised its other hand and extended its index finger towards the foul-looking drink. The end of UMA's finger suddenly lit up with a sharp white light, his yellow eyes started to flicker, and the white fingertip-light grew brighter and stronger.

Robert could hear a low, throbbing electronic-like sound coming from UMA as the robot now pointed at the cocktail glass filled with its disgusting ingredients. He dipped his illuminated finger into the dirty contents of the glass, which lit it up and revealed that a few dead insects were floating in the drink he was preparing. Suddenly, the light grew intensely bright, and Robert had to close his eyes because it felt like he was looking directly at the sun.

The throbbing sounds coming from UMA suddenly stopped, and Robert opened one eye to peek at the scene before him. Standing before him was a proud-looking UMA holding a large and quite fantastic-looking cocktail drink! The cocktail glass was now filled with a fizzing icy blue liquid, and perched on it rested a dazzling orange-petalled flower that smelled of a freshly picked satsuma. It looked incredible.

"So, *that's* a UMA Satsuma Surprise?" asked Robert quietly.

UMA nodded twice and quickly turned and brought the drink out to Robert's mother, who was now busy ordering a sun lounger pillow that could give her a head massage. Robert stood still in the shed as he heard his mother try the cocktail drink. It was a few long seconds before Robert heard her annoying weaselly voice squeal, "Delish, delish, delish! You've done it again, my metal mate! It's absolutely gorge! I can taste the Satsoooma for little Consooma. I am so glad you are here, little man. I won't need to lift a finger with you around to look after me, my little metal pickle!"

On hearing this, Robert jumped out from the garden shed door and headed straight to the patio area to confront his annoying mother.

"No chance, Mum! UMA is not your house slave, and he certainly doesn't belong to you!"

Robert's anger grew even more when his mother responded with a giggle and a snort. She looked at Robert and shook her head slowly, peering over her designer sunglasses as she sipped from her cocktail. She finished the drink in one last greedy gulp before saying, "Oh, Robert, just listen to yourself. Don't you know these robots are just plain stupid and here to serve? He has done everything I have told him today, and I can't wait for him to start building me my own little snack bar with its own private health spa. He's a great cook too! Your daddy bought him for me, and he knows how much I like getting spoilt."

For once, Robert refused to react to his mother. He calmly walked to UMA, who was standing dutifully by the side of his mother's sun lounger, and took UMA by the hand. "Come on, UMA. No one deserves to be a slave to anyone."

His mother sniggered and cackled to herself as Robert and UMA left the garden. As she laughed, she realised she needed to re-order some anti-wobble belly cream.

6
The Baccinos

Lilly Baccino stood at her open back door, looking out over her garden that she had worked and nurtured for sixty years. She could clearly remember how the garden had first looked when she and her husband arrived in a cold and chilly England, coming from their small and much warmer village in Italy. The garden had been a large field of dirty, soggy soil and mud hills.

Now, it was a lush and handsome garden, which proudly featured an old red-brick path that curled its way to the end of the garden, which sat perched over the canal. Lilly enjoyed standing on the small wooden deck that sat between the garden and the gentle calm canal waters, waving to the passing boats and barges. Without thinking, she would smile and raise her hand at passing strangers, who would always respond to her greeting with an eager smile and a willing wave. Sometimes the canal people stopped to talk and ask for something they needed – most often they requested fresh water for a dog that would be sitting and panting on the barge roof. Lilly was always happy to smile and help anybody. She often wondered why people didn't smile and wave to each other in the city. Maybe those city people were just too smart or too busy for that type of stuff?

She moved her gaze from the canal deck to the familiar figure struggling and mumbling at the edge of the garden. It was her husband, Dennis Baccino, pulling at some annoying overgrown hedges that poked out over the manicured lawn. Lilly giggled as his mumbles and grumbles grew louder while he wrestled more forcefully at the branches, still failing to pull them from the hedge. Her giggles evolved to a full chuckle as Dennis pulled so hard at the hedge branch, it stubbornly jerked back and slipped through his hands (Dennis didn't bother with gardening gloves). She laughed out loud as Dennis fell and rolled over backwards on the dewy lawn. He lay silently on the grass, looking like he was demonstrating a lie-down star jump, his 88-year-old body spread-eagled as he looked up at the denim blue sky. He could hear Lilly's bellowing laugh, and while retaining his horizontal position and remaining quite still, he shouted, "Uffa! Ha, ha, ha! Hilarious, Lilly. Hilarious! I could be seriously injured here, and you are laughing and pointing like a silly village girl!"

Lilly stopped for a millisecond to process what Dennis had just said, and this only made her laugh out even more, this time reaching a louder whooping chortle as she tried to cover her mouth.

"*Mamma mia*, Lilly! *Basta*! No more of the funny giggle stuff! I am too old for falling over like a silly circus clown!" Dennis rambled on with both hands now gesticulating in a typically Italian way while he stared up at the cloudless sky. The shadow of Lilly slowly covered his face, and as he looked up, he could see the familiar outline of her head and shoulders standing above him, still shaking with a restrained effort to stop laughing at the old Italian man lying star-shaped on the damp grass.

Dennis had hesitated for a few moments before then starting to snigger. He could never be mad at his darling Lilly for too long, and he could always eventually laugh at his short-fused temper. He looked up seriously at Lilly and whispered, "*Avviso bagnato bum*! Wet bum alert, wet bum alert!"

Then they joined together in a burst of hearty laughter. They both smiled as Lilly helped her old husband up to his feet and walked him slowly to the wooden canal deck at the end of the garden.

Dennis enjoyed sitting in his old barber's chair, which he had rescued from an old barbershop that was shutting down. It was an old, classic chair which boasted the finest leather and still swivelled up, down, and around, without a sound on the decking. Mrs Baccino enjoyed a more typical leather armchair, which was filled with comfy cushions. Both of the chairs faced the placid waters, and as they both creaked into their comfortable seats, Lilly still giggled as she added, "What a wonderful anniversary present that would be! Elderly husband dies on his wedding anniversary following fight with garden hedge!" They both snickered at the imaginary newspaper headline.

Lilly continued, "What *shall* we do to commemorate our sixtieth wedding anniversary?" She surveyed up and down the empty canal as she waited for an answer from her husband. She waited a few minutes before turning to see her husband catnapping in the morning sun. "Dennis! *Mio Dio*! You don't take your nap until 3 p.m., and it's only eleven o'clock! Wake up, you old fool! We haven't even had lunch yet, and I was talking to you!"

Dennis rolled his head from one side to another, his eyes still closed, but hiding a half-smile on his wrinkled face. "Sorry, darling, what was that?"

Lilly tutted and folded her arms as she repeated, "I said before you rudely dozed off – what shall we do to mark our wedding anniversary?" Again, she patiently waited for his response.

"How about observing a minute's silence?" Dennis joked before reaching out to take Lilly's hand.

They both howled with laughter as a canal barge quietly cruised by with a soft engine hum, just ten feet away from the laughing old couple sitting on the canal-side. They continued to laugh as the barge passed by; the barge pilot (a man with a salt-and-pepper-coloured bushy beard and a ship skipper's hat) stared at them with a puzzled smile.

He and his barge quietly hummed away from view, while Dennis and Lilly still teetered in their comfortable chairs. The old Italian couple sat at an old oak table, where they would usually place the Baccino family teapot for mid-morning tea and biscuits, red wine, and salad in the afternoon, and pasta with warm bread and a mug of cocoa for supper. In the middle of the table was a large bowl of fresh fruit, which was always replenished each morning by Lilly. They would always snack on various fruits through the day as they relaxed by the canal-side. Most days they would work in the garden, read books and newspapers, and listen to the radio while Lilly would knit and Dennis mulled over a sudoku or crossword puzzle.

Often, they would talk about life. The past, the present and the future. Occasionally, they would dance when it was sunny. It reminded them of when they had danced back in Italy when they were young. Dennis and Lilly had first danced together when they were just fourteen years old. It was at a large family wedding, and the whole village celebrated in the local square. Lilly's older sister was the bride that day, and Lilly was the young bridesmaid, dressed in elegant, pure white lace.

Dennis could still remember being transfixed by Lilly that day, and he could still hear the laughs and jokes from his teasing young friends as he walked from one side of the village square to the other, never taking his eyes away from her. It was the first time he'd thought a girl could look truly beautiful. As he reached Lilly on the other side of the old village square, and before he even said a word to her, Lilly had whispered, "*Si*, Dennis." She took his nervous hand and they joined the wedding dance floor in the old dusty square. She didn't even notice the other girls point and whisper as she danced that day.

The old Symphola gramophone player sat on the oak table behind the fruit bowl. It was timeworn and heavy but had never failed to play for its owners. It still required winding up before it could make its tinny sound, and while both Lilly and Dennis knew the sound quality wasn't brilliant, or very loud, the sounds of that gramophone never failed to transport both of them back to the village square back in Italy. It was the very same gramophone player that had played its soft music to that very first dance many years before. That same old gramophone was a wedding gift to Dennis and Lilly, from the residents of the small village they lived in. Once they married, Dennis and Lilly left to explore the big and wonderful world that awaited them.

Dennis leant forward and placed his old hand on the even older gramophone handle, and with a delicate touch, gently turned the handle several times before lifting the gramophone arm and carefully resting its needle on the old vinyl disc that lay on the rotating turntable. The gramophone speaker made a crackly echo sound before the familiar sounds of dreamy Italian orchestra strings flowed out from the machine.

Lilly smiled as she looked up at Dennis, standing before her with an outstretched hand. Before he could even say a word, she nodded. "*Si*, Dennis. *Sempre*."

They slowly danced on the canal deck, oblivious to any of the passing chugging canal barges. They didn't notice the twelve-year-old girl watching them from the round attic window in the roof of the tall Baccino house. The girl touched the cold window glass as she looked down at her grandparents dancing together in the garden, wanting to feel the happiness that they shared at that moment. She almost smiled as they danced and laughed, but somehow resisted. She then picked up her pencil and began to draw the happy old Italian couple as they danced below her. She noticed the large damp patch on the seat of her granddad's trousers. Again, she felt compelled to laugh out loud but decided to keep it inside for now.

Young Velia Rose Baccino *always* kept things to herself.

7
Breaking News

YAMANUCHI ROBOTICS

"Consooma, darling! Time to go, honey pie, the engine's running and we'll need to refuel again – all those shops are waiting for you, sweetie!" Keith Karma called from the hallway.

He shouted again as he fixated his eyes on his large mobile device, its blue glow shining a pale light on its owner's fat and puffy face, the screen reflecting on his thick, round spectacles.

"Satnav. Check. Double parking space reservation. Check. All-you-can-eat buffet booked. Check. If only I could schedule my toilet breaks, then everything could be totally organised. Ah well, someone can develop an app for that. A gap in the market opportunity."

Consooma Karma rolled down the stairs like a soft damp ball of flabby dough. She heavily thudded down each stair step, which in turn provided an unintentional slow drum beat as she reached the bottom of the stairs. She was dressed to impress and had painted her face with her expensive (but totally ineffective) makeup that promised to make her look ten years younger. She looked ten years older. She checked her look in the large mirror in the hallway and nodded approvingly at her appearance as she muttered, "Hope you've got a full wallet today, Keith Karma. I have a real need for some high-intensive consumer therapy. Going to give it large, so brace yourself and those credit cards!"

Her husband nodded immediately and returned a weak smile. "Yes, dear. No use in me working all hours if we can't enjoy it, eh? I made a shopping checklist on my phone. Just the seventy-one items to get today including the designer bin bags you spotted on the shopping channel – you know the ones, with the perfume-scented pink polythene and pink silk tie handles." Robert's parents wobbled out from the front door, continuing to run through the list of items they would acquire but didn't need.

Robert watched them approach the vehicle that was gently throbbing and spewing out its engine smoke around the driveway. The vehicle was too big to be classed as a car and much too small to be called a truck, but either way, it was the ugliest and clunkiest automobile Robert had ever seen. His mother had selected a customised pale acid-lemon colour to match her favourite gloves, and the vehicle also included hyped-up suspension and tractor-like tyres to give it a pronounced and ridiculous height.

Robert shook his head as he watched his mother attempting to pull herself up into the passenger seat, which required the use of three side-door steps. His mother could not quite pull herself into the vehicle, and so his dad had to shove and nudge at her huge and flabby backside to assist her boarding. It looked like his father was trying to bulldoze a bouncy castle into the car door, and Robert cringed in embarrassment as his mother eventually sat, perched, on the seat.

Consooma Karma half-smiled to herself, happy now she could enjoy looking down at the other cars as they made their way to the shops while she enjoyed the dominant view. The large chunky car slowly rolled out of the driveway, moving like a military tank (and demanding as much fuel). Robert and UMA stood at the lounge bay window, both shaking their heads.

"They'll have fun trying to park that thing in town," Robert scoffed as his parents disappeared from view under a fog of sooty exhaust smoke. He turned to look down at UMA, who was standing at his side. The small robot had placed his metal hands on his robotic hips and was looking eagerly up at his new best friend, waiting to receive a task or instruction. Robert peered into UMA's yellow eyes and wondered just what the robot was thinking.

"Well, pal, that's the horrible parents out of the way for a few hours. Thought maybe we could go out ourselves, get some fresh air in those metal lungs of yours?"

UMA didn't respond and remained silent as he carefully studied Robert's face. The robot then lowered his head and raised a hand to his circular chest light as it produced a hazy blue glow. This slightly surprised Robert, as he had only ever seen the chest light illuminate a red blush.

"Something you want to tell me, UMA?" Robert asked as UMA shrugged and remained still, his blue glow quietly pulsing on his chest. Robert somehow sensed sadness and placed his hand on the robot's shoulder. "You can tell me. I want to help you, UMA. Best friends, remember?"

UMA lifted his head to face Robert and the robot's big yellow glass eyes brightened and fluttered. He turned and walked to the large wall-mounted plasma TV, which resembled a dark rectangular black mirror. Although the TV was switched off, UMA raised his hand, and as had happened when he made his magic cocktail, his index finger started to glow with a bright white light. The robot moved its glowing finger to the side of the plasma TV and inserted his finger into one of the several connection ports located on the side panel. Immediately, the TV came to life, and its screen blinked into a grainy image as some crackling sound came from the speakers.

Robert stood before the images being broadcast, his little robot companion remaining on tiptoes with his finger still inserted in the TV set, arching his head to view the TV bulletin that had just started. It was an international news clip with the familiar red and white "BREAKING NEWS" message scrolling along the bottom of the screen.

The image featured the face of an old Chinese man who had a bald head and a wispy grey beard. Robert looked at the man's eyes and thought they reflected kindness. The room filled with a blue glow as UMA's chest light emitted a bright pulsating glow as he looked up at the man on the TV screen.

The news presenter then made the following announcement: "And that breaking news for you again – the father of modern robotics and the richest man in the world, Changpu Yamanuchi, has disappeared. The seventy-year-old founder of Yamanuchi Robotics has lived a reclusive life and is understood to have spent the last eight years of his life working alone in his private laboratory trying to pioneer robotic AE: Artificial Emotion. He has not been seen for six months."

Robert and UMA watched as the news presenter continued to talk while some older images appeared on the screen. The words "library archive images" flashed slowly in the bottom corner of the screen as the newscaster continued, "Let's take a look at Changpu Yamanuchi's extraordinary life of achievement . . ."

Some old black-and-white images opened the news clip, which showed an old black-and-white photo of a happy fisherman standing proudly with a smiling young boy, both of then holding up the catch of the day.

"Changpu Yamanuchi was raised in a small fishing village on the eastern coast of China. Young Changpu idolised his father and went out fishing with his dad every day and learned much about life. They were thought to be inseparable. Changpu enjoyed a simple and happy upbringing until his father found work in a new local car factory. His father worked eighteen hours a day and slept at employee facilities in the factory. He was only allowed monthly home visits. His father's enforced absence significantly damaged the Yamanuchi family and sadly caused his parents to separate. This event devastated the family and inspired his intelligent young son, Changpu, to invent and develop a new generation of robots that could perform the work his father had to do in the factory. His goal was to automate the work at the plant and release his father from such demanding work so they could once again be a happy family and return to a simple fisherman's life. Changpu founded Yamanuchi Robotics, and soon his pioneering robots were developed and then mass produced and deployed with great success."

The black-and-white grainy TV images then showed thousands of robots stood in organised lines, all of them looking just like UMA. The only difference Robert could detect was that the robots on the TV screen did not have any circular chest light. His mouth was agape at the images showing massive car production lines, all containing hundreds of robots working like busy worker ants on the production line, quickly and efficiently manufacturing new cars.

The newscaster continued talking over the news clip. "The introduction of robotic technology soon resulted in his father and all of his colleagues losing their jobs at the local factory. Many people blamed the Yamanuchi family for the job losses, and Changpu's father was ashamed that his very own son was behind the introduction of mass-scale robotics. His father was angered and disowned his son in a fury and disappeared. Changpu was left alone at a very young age and is thought to have then devoted his life to robotic development, consequently becoming the richest man in the world. He is often reported as the most world's most successful man and is understood to have amassed an estimated personal fortune of 783 trillion dollars."

The images changed and a screen presentation listed all the different industries that used Yamanuchi Robotics: cars, trains, aircraft, electronics, computers, mobile phones, televisions, satellites. The news item continued.

"Changpu Yamanuchi never married or had a family and disappeared from any public life eight years ago. It's thought he was developing a new advanced generation of robot, but it is not known if he succeeded in doing this before his disappearance. In his last interview, recorded many years ago, Mr Yamanuchi had this to say . . ."

The news clip then displayed an interview with the old man in his private robotics lab. In the background, Robert could see two UMA-like robot heads on a lab bench, close to the body of a robot that was attached to a prop stand on the lab bench. The robot's body featured a circular chest light unit, which was being tested on a lab bench. It had many wires feeding into it, and the circular chest sphere was flashing an alternate red and blue glow. There were robot parts all around the lab, and Robert even noticed some hands and feet that looked the same as UMA's. The old man spoke in a slow and gentle voice, his eyes still looking shiny and alive with a bright intensity for such an old man.

"Life used to be very simple. People had much less but seemed happier and enjoyed being together. Then big industry came, and the factories took many people away, including my father. I invented robots to do all the hard work. I thought that this would then allow the people to come together and be free again . . . but I was wrong. People did not come together, and they seemed to separate from each other. It now seems people only want to be alone, to get lost in work and technology, just acquiring things for themselves.

"I think we are losing the ability to connect as humans. I am the richest man in the world, but I am not a successful person, as I have realised that I don't have the most precious things in life. People need to learn to love and feel human again. Other robotic companies are developing AI (Artificial Intelligence), and this is easily possible, as all intelligence is based on data, information, and programmable rules. The real breakthrough will be the discovery of AE: Artificial Emotion. Only then can we really understand how unique human feelings are."

UMA disconnected his finger from the TV set and stepped back to stand alongside Robert, both of them now looking at a large blank plasma screen.

"The man in that news clip," began Robert, "did you know him, UMA?"

The small robot slowly lowered his head and nodded as his chest light shone with a dull blue light this time. The robot placed both of his hands over the chest light, as if to try to hide its cool glow, his small internal motors making a quiet whirring sound.

"Who is he?" asked Robert in a low voice.

UMA hesitated and then walked towards the wall in the lounge that was decorated with various framed family photos. Sitting proudly in the centre of the pictures was a large framed photo that was titled "Employee of the Month: Keith Karma – 42,576 emails sent." The photo featured Robert's father with two incredibly massive thumbs raised above his mobile device and his telephone headset attached to his head as he wore the most annoying swaggering smirk. Robert had forgotten how ridiculous the photo looked, and then he realised what UMA was trying to tell him.

"Father? Father! I understand, UMA. That man on the TV, Mr Yamanuchi, is he your father?"

The little robot stood at the bay window and produced another bright bloom of red glow as he nodded. UMA really missed his father. He loved him so much.

8
The Girl at the Attic Window

The girl at the attic window looked down at her neighbour's house. She had been staring at the ground-floor bay window, which had been making a strange red and blue glow. Unusually for her, she found the colours fascinating and almost hypnotic.

Velia Rose Baccino had lived with her grandparents for nearly three years. Her parents had accepted an exciting career opportunity which involved them travelling around the world making specialist documentary films. They were so busy that they didn't ever find time to come home. They sent an occasional postcard from places Velia Rose had never heard of, but the postcards eventually stopped arriving. They did try to use a computer for a video call once, but her grandparents didn't understand how to set it all up. Besides, even if they *could* connect via the computer, it wouldn't be much use, as Velia Rose didn't talk any more.

It was just something she stopped doing – a bit like when she stopped sleeping with her favourite teddy bear. Velia Rose remembered being taken to see some special kind of doctor in the city. She could recall Granny Lilly crying into a handkerchief as she listened to the doctor, and she remembered reading the words "**selective mute**" written on the top of a paper form that sat on the doctor's desk. The doctor had given Granny three booklets and offered a good luck smile and a sympathetic handshake as they left the appointment that day.

Granny Lilly hadn't said a word on the train home that day. For a few hours, Velia Rose had thought they were both selective mutes as they silently watched the passing countryside from the window of the train on that dark overcast night.

Velia Rose spent all of her time in her bedroom attic. It was her favourite room in the house because she could see so much from her attic windows. She liked the peace and quietness of being so high above all of the noise and bustle on the streets. She much preferred observing life rather than taking part in it.

Best of all, she could draw and paint – not regular drawings that most kids could create, but incredibly detailed lifelike drawings that she created from her memory. Granddad had researched her skill; it was called photorealism. She had a photographic memory and found it quite natural to recreate a drawing from whatever she could recall in her mind. Granny Lilly and Granddad Dennis were always amazed at her drawings and paintings. They would take each piece of work to the attic window and compare reality with whatever Velia Rose had created on the paper, and they usually said the same thing. "Wow! It's exactly the same! *Di preciso*! Just like a photograph. Amazing! Just . . . *fantastico*!"

Usually, they would then turn to Velia Rose and ask her how she could create such wonderful pieces, but they had now got pretty used to her typical response, which would be a polite but silent half-smile. All her drawings were black and white, with occasional shades of charcoal greys. Sometimes the drawings were of the surrounding buildings, each minute brick detail correctly copied from her mind, and sometimes the picture would feature a tree, or a bird, or a neighbour. They were all recreated in incredible detail, which made the drawings look real, beautiful, and sometimes sad.

A few years back, her grandparents had bought her professional artist pencils, which included thirty-two coloured shaded pencils, but the large wooden pencil box still lay unopened. For now, her mind and her life felt very black and white.

Velia Rose turned her gaze from her neighbour's window and looked around her attic bedroom. It got cold up in the attic, but she had got used to that. Most of the walls were covered in the many black-and-white drawings she had made from memory. One of the walls she kept clear was strictly reserved for any letters or postcards she might receive from her parents. This wall made her sad, as the few postcards or letters pinned to the wall just covered a small corner area. She looked at her drawings again – each drawing was a snapshot in time, and they hung on the walls like ghosts from the past.

Velia Rose returned her gaze to the neighbour's window, but this time she caught her breath as she realised someone – or *something* – was staring right back up at her. Its pale yellow eyes pulsed as it slowly raised its hand and waved at her. Velia Rose jerked quickly away as she ducked below the window, out of sight and away from the daylight. Her heart jumped as she realised someone had noticed her watching from her window in the sky. She dared not appear at the window for at least another hour, by that time the weird thing that was looking up at her would probably have disappeared.

She huddled below the windowsill, hidden from view, and kept thinking about what she had seen. Many times before, Velia Rose had looked at the neighbour's house and had only ever noticed the lonely boy, sitting alone in his bedroom, doing jobs around the house, or hanging around his garden. She found the boy interesting and had even made a few drawings of him. Of course, the boy didn't know of this. The boy didn't even know about the girl in the attic window.

Now, though, she was puzzled and intrigued about the new neighbour. While she was still hidden from view and crouched on her bedroom floor, she took her pencils and started drawing in her sketchbook. Quickly and very skilfully, she drew from her memory to recreate the image that was still vivid in her mind. The drawing was so detailed and lifelike that after twenty minutes it looked like a black-and-white photograph.

She looked carefully into the robot's eyes that she had just recreated on the paper before her, looking below his face to his chest, which she recalled had burned with a bright red light. For the first time in her life, Velia Rose reached across to the dusty box of pencils and slowly opened the wooden box, tracing her finger along the rainbow spectrum row of pencils until she stopped at the red one. She didn't know why, but for some reason, she now wanted some colour in her life. She continued working on her drawing, adding a radiant red misty glow around the robot. She was so immersed in her drawing that she had not noticed she was now wearing a broad smile on her face. It was the kind of smile she had always kept inside.

9
The Accidental Job Interview

Robert felt the need to get out of the house and decided to take UMA for a walk along the nearby banks of the canal. He enjoyed the surprised looks from a few of the old salty sea-dog barge pilots when they spotted a boy and a robot walking happily along the canal-side. They still raised a friendly hand to wave at the passing strangers, but Robert could tell they were amazed at seeing UMA. They were even more amazed when UMA stopped to wave back with great enthusiasm. UMA seemed to have a connection with some of the dogs that sat on the barge tops, as every dog jumped and wagged its tail excitedly when they got close.

Robert was quite familiar with the canal, and he would often take walks along it as an attractive alternative to sitting in the house and being shouted at by his greedy, selfish parents. He and the robot walked along the canal and came to an open area of water that widened up to allow the barges to turn. There was a small cafe kiosk here, and it was possible to rent a small rowing boat for thirty-minute sessions.

"You ever been on the water, UMA?" Robert asked as they stood looking at some ducks paddling along the canal.

The robot nodded its head but looked a bit unsure of the water. Robert wasn't entirely sure if letting a robot go near water was a good idea, as he was pretty sure UMA would have some serious electronics inside his small metal case. Electronics and water were not usually a good combination. All the same, he had hired a boat ride many times before and always felt quite lonely sitting alone in a two-man boat.

"Boat ride for two, please," Robert said cheerfully to the grumpy-looking man in the kiosk. The kiosk man passed two boat oars over the counter and, without losing his inquisitive gaze, which firmly locked on UMA, he glumly stated, "Thirty minutes only. No messing around."

***

Dennis Baccino loved his garden. He quite enjoyed the gardening work because it gave him some physical exercise, but most of all, he gained great satisfaction from creating something beautiful that others could also enjoy. He loved watching the garden change through the seasons. Whatever season it was, Dennis had planned and cultivated the garden so expertly that there was always something that was in full bloom of dazzling colour. He was busy pruning flowers today, and he was working on a begonia bush nestled just by the deck area that sat between the garden and canal.

The gramophone was playing an old classical waltz, and Dennis hummed the tune as he swayed his hips to the sweeping violins playing from the old machine. He looked back at his house and could see his wife at the kitchen window. Lilly was busy fixing lunch, and Dennis knew it would be a delicious traditional Italian salad, and that it would be ready in the next ten minutes. He felt a slight twinge in his right shoulder, and his right hand that was holding the pruner tool suddenly felt weak.

"Just two more stems to prune before lunch, old son," Dennis said to himself.

Although he was starting to feel a bit queasy, Dennis wanted to finish the job so he could enjoy his lunch and then take a nap in the mild afternoon. Suddenly, though, the twinge in his shoulder became a sudden and severe pain, and Dennis dropped his pruning tool as he moved both clutching hands to his upper chest. He wanted to shout out for Lilly, but the only noise he could muster was a low groan as he fell to his knees by the canal-side. Dizziness and blurred vision made the begonia bush in front of him seem like a dark wall of green. The pain in his chest became stifling, and Dennis was now struggling to breathe. He keeled over backwards, falling into the canal, slowly submerging into the cold and dark waters. The daylight disappeared as he drifted below the surface of the water. Everything was fading now, and Dennis felt like a long deep sleep would soon follow. So weak . . . getting darker . . . getting colder . . . so tired.

Under the water, Dennis fell into a deep, heavy sleep, and in his dream, he was dancing again in the moonlight. Lilly and Velia Rose joined him, and all three of them connected in a small triangle as they swayed to the music. They all smiled and danced as they moved to the sounds of warming music. *Maybe this was heaven? Not bad*, he thought, as he danced with his two darling girls. As he looked up, the round milky-white moon shone brightly in his face. It moved closer and closer, and even in the dream, Dennis squinted his eyes as the moonlight intensified. Except that it wasn't moonlight, and it wasn't a dream.

UMA's hand reached down from the rowing boat into the canal waters, his index finger shining fiercely as he searched for the old man in the water. The light was as bright as a lighthouse beam, so powerful that Robert could see it illuminating the murky waters of the canal. He could see fish swim away to escape the radiation of light and thought he even spotted an old bicycle lying on the bed of the canal. Most clearly, though, he could see the body of the old man.

Without a moment's hesitation, Robert dived into the water to reach the still figure. The following few moments lasted a long time in his mind, as he reached the old man and took a firm hold of him before pushing up, back towards the surface of the water. Except Robert could now not reach the surface. He struggled and pushed several times to try to move upwards, but he remained holding on to the old man within the silent, dark depths. Robert felt like he was being pulled under by a giant metal claw, clutching his leg and restraining him at the bottom of the canal. He was struggling, and the effort to hold on to the old man as well as getting back above the water's surface was incredible. He could feel the light fading fast.

A metal arm reached into the water, and its hand took hold of the old man's cardigan and pulled him out from the water and on to the canal bank. The little robot immediately returned to the water and firmly clutched on to the young boy, who was now frantically thrashing around as he fought for breath. The robot's hand found the boy's arm and promptly and firmly pulled him. But the robot could not lift him from the water – something was holding the boy down.

The robot went below and realised quickly that Robert's leg had become tangled in the frame of an old bicycle wreck that sat on the canal bed. The robot delved further below the water, and with a calm and rapid expertise, produced a small circular saw from another metal finger. With one hand, the robot shone its bright light on to the bicycle, while with its other hand, it expertly cut away at the old rusted metal of the bike frame, instantly releasing Robert from its tangle. The robot held the boy as they quickly propelled upwards to safety.

Robert reached the water's surface and found the strength to climb on to the wooden deck at the edge of the canal. He was joined by UMA as they both quickly moved to attend to the old unconscious man. Robert could hear a blend of classical music and the screams of a woman as UMA examined the old man.

The screams got nearer as UMA held out his small metal hand, and once again a metal finger flipped back to reveal another useful tool. This time, a red electrical prong instantly appeared from the base of the robot's finger, and UMA quickly ripped open the old man's wet shirt and placed the prong device on his chest. Robert stared as the robot's finger buzzed and vibrated, and he assumed the tool could act as a defibrillator. He was right, as within seconds, the old man's body jolted as the robot attempted to kick-start the muscles of his heart. The old lady now stood above her husband, holding her face in terror as her husband struggled to find life.

"Dennis? Dennis! What's happening? What have you done, Dennis? He can't swim! Help him! Save him, please! *Il Mio Amore!*" cried Lilly as she kneeled at the side of her still husband. She could only stare as UMA continued to hold his finger on her husband's chest.

Only then did she realise that the finger had belonged to a small and careful robot, and she cried, "We need a real doctor, not some robot! Get a doctor, get an ambulance! *Veloce!*" The old woman sobbed as she squeezed her husband's cold, wet hand, until she heard a familiar voice.

"Careful, Lill, you'll snap my hand off if you squeeze it any tighter." Dennis lay there, looking at his wife, his eyes smiling at her, his face and grey hair still soaking wet.

Lilly buried her head into his chest as she sobbed with tears of relief. Dennis looked beyond his wife's trembling shoulder and up at the strange figures that looked down at him. He recognised the boy – for it was the boy who lived next door, the quiet lad with the busy, silly parents. Dennis didn't know the smaller figure with the glowing red chest and bright yellow eyes. He wasn't sure if he was still in that strange dream but soon felt better once he sat in his comfortable garden chair with a thick bath towel around his shoulders and a mug of hot milky tea in his hands.

"You are not a high-priority call, Dennis!" called Lilly Baccino as she walked to him with a telephone still held to her ear. "They will come in the next few hours. They say you are not an emergency if you can sit up, talk, and drink milky tea. *Mamma Mia!*" Lilly rolled her eyes but looked lovingly at her husband, her face still resisting breaking into a smile of relief.

Dennis was sitting in his garden chair, and both Robert and UMA stood next to him, both very relieved and quietly proud that they had helped save the old man. Dennis started to chuckle and nodded as he mumbled, "I thought I was a goner then. Thought that was it." His eyes looked frightened at the very thought before he tried to improve the mood by adding, "Still, no time for slacking . . . need to finish pruning those begonias—". His gaze met Lily's shocked and fiery expression.

"No way, Dennis! You are not doing anything! It's rest and more rest for you. I think this is God's way of telling you that your gardening days are over. It's a miracle you didn't die! These boys saved your life."

Dennis looked up and down at the small robot standing timidly in front of him. He looked at the robot's hands but could not see any tools at the end of its metal fingertips now. He continued to focus on the robot and said, "Certainly was a miracle, love. I really don't know how to thank you both."

The old man smiled at Robert and UMA. Lilly placed her hands on Dennis and playfully ruffled his grey hair. She said, "Don't worry, love. We can get some professional gardeners in. We can make a few savings here and there to find the money. They can do all the spadework from now on. I'll look for a reliable gardening company, don't worry. You rest up."

But Lilly didn't have to worry about looking for new gardeners for long. She looked over at Dennis, who was already smiling as he pointed. She followed his finger to see the sweet, quiet boy from next door raking some leaves on the lawn, while his small robot friend stood at a lush flower bed, an old tin watering can in his hand as he quietly and carefully sprayed water over some blossoming tulips. Both Dennis and Lilly smiled, the old man chuckling as he shouted over to them, "Hey, boys, you got the job!"

10
Angel Bait

That summer, Robert and UMA spent most of their time together and became the best of friends. *True soul mates.* Robert was always amazed by his little metallic companion. First, UMA was mega-efficient in that he could perform so many jobs in quick and reliable ways. He never seemed to stop! During the night, the robot would silently clean the house and prepare food for the following day; sometimes he would even go out in the cold night and clean and valet Mr Karma's ugly car. UMA kept the house ultra-tidy and kept Robert's parents quiet by providing a steady stream of tea, cake, and biscuits.

Robert had read on the Internet that Yamanuchi Robotics was the only company in the world to utilise perpetual motion technology. He didn't understand the scientific jargon behind all of this but knew that this meant UMA didn't require any external energy source to keep him active. UMA just kept on going and always seemed happy to help anyone.

UMA wasn't moving around all the time, however. Every day, UMA would sit at Robert's laptop for at least a few hours. Robert didn't understand what UMA was doing, but it always involved him quietly tapping away on the keyboard and viewing Internet pages with Chinese writing and map images. Robert assumed UMA's favourite subject was geography.

The two friends did everything you would expect two regular best friends to do, especially playing together in the fresh outdoors. Robert had never had a true friend before, and the happy times with UMA made him forget about the time before UMA arrived when Robert was mostly alone. Now that Robert spent most of his time with UMA, his parents became even less interested in him. They seemed happier to be consumed by TV, working too much, eating too much food, drinking too much wine, buying stuff they didn't need, and mostly ignoring each other. Robert almost felt pity for them, but as they were fully grown adults, they should know better, he thought. UMA didn't understand Robert's parents. They were lucky enough to have a family but didn't appear to embrace it.

Things were very different in the Baccino garden. Robert and UMA made a small gate in the back garden hedges so they could easily enter their neighbour's garden every morning. For the first month, they just went through to do the gardening with the idea of just taking over the work that Mr Baccino could no longer perform, but things seemed to evolve from there. Lilly and Dennis Baccino were so kind-hearted and grateful to Robert and UMA that they regarded their new gardeners like adopted sons.

Robert and UMA loved working in the garden while the old couple played old music, joked, and laughed, and always kept delicious, healthy refreshments coming through the day. In return, the scope of the garden project changed a bit. Instead of maintaining the garden, Robert and UMA presented some elegant and beautiful garden designs to make it even better. That summer, the happy gardeners created a new herb garden (which Lilly used for her brilliant cooking) and they planted new flower bushes that would naturally diffuse the garden with aromatic scents, which reminded the old Italian couple of their hometown. UMA made a spectacular garden fountain, which featured a mesmerising waterfall with jets of water that would spurt from the surface of the water and seemed to dance around the fountain pool. At the centre of the fountain was a small podium, on which stood a lifelike statue of a lone fisherman, looking out into the distance with a ship's wheel in his hands. The podium even rotated slowly as the fountain flowed, allowing the lone statue to survey every direction, searching for something continually. Everyone loved the fountain, especially the girl in the attic window.

Even though Velia Rose had not left her attic bedroom in the first few sunny months of summer, she had been fascinated to watch the two new gardeners transform the garden into a small private paradise. Every day, she watched the boy and the robot add something new to the garden, and whatever it was, she would capture it in a remarkable lifelike colour drawing. She had even started painting and had already pinned several outstanding watercolours on to the walls of the attic.

Best of all, every drawing or painting she did included Robert. The little robot fascinated her, but there was just something about Robert. Velia Rose didn't understand it, but she knew she felt happier when Robert arrived every day to work in the garden.

Creating drawings and paintings of him gave her an excellent excuse to look at him from her single window in the sky. Every day, she opened the attic windows and enjoyed the sound of his distant voice and warm laughter coming from below her room. Every day, the little robot would stop working for a moment and stare up at the window, hoping to see the girl in the window. But Robert wasn't even aware that he was being admired.

Lilly Baccino sat on the edge of Velia Rose's bed and delighted herself in looking at the interesting, colourful works that covered the walls of the attic. Even though Velia Rose had not left her room for a few years, Lilly could feel a change in her granddaughter. Lilly and Dennis loved Velia Rose very much, but it hurt them that she was so withdrawn from the world. They just wanted their granddaughter to be happy. They felt helpless that they could not control the situation, and it also pained them that Velia Rose's parents had made the decision to follow their busy careers rather than be there for their daughter. Every day, her small and old grandmother would climb several stories of stairs to reach her granddaughter in the attic room. Every day, she would say the same thing to Velia Rose. "But you must come down and say hello to the boys! They are so friendly, and they work so hard. They are about to take a break and it would nice if you could come say hello?"

Lilly would never accept that Velia Rose might not ever talk again. "Please, darling, for your grandmother? Please come out into the garden, feel the sun, and smell the flowers? Please stop hiding from life."

Every day, Velia Rose would shake her head while reaching to hug her grandmother. She didn't want to hurt her grandmother's feelings, but somehow she felt lost, and the only place that made sense to her was the attic bedroom.

Robert and UMA enjoyed spending their days at the Baccinos – so much so, they didn't feel as if they were working. They felt like they were living. They refused to take any money from their old neighbours but gladly accepted the many refreshments they received through the day to keep them energised. It occurred to Robert that he had never felt better. He was eating well, getting plenty of fresh air and sunshine, and he realised he didn't need to spend any money to feel so good.

Of course, UMA never drank or snacked on biscuit or cake. Whenever Robert took a break, UMA would stand by the fountain and either look up at the statue of the fisherman or stare up at the

Baccinos' house, for some reason.

Robert and UMA wondered about what next addition they could make to the Baccinos' garden, and Robert wasn't totally surprised when UMA ran to the house and returned with a design he had apparently made during the night while everyone slept.

The little robot unrolled the paper to reveal a very impressive blueprint design of a summer house. It was a round building and featured many circular windows and doors. The wooden roof gently rose to its peak, and instead of a chimney poking through the top of the roof, there was a small lighthouse that seemed to look just perfect.

Robert nodded approvingly. "Very impressive, UMA, but why a summer house? A bit of an ambitious project, don't you think?"

The little robot pulled out another piece of blank paper, lifted one hand, and revealed a finger, which then produced a pencil tip from its end. The little robot began scribbling on the paper. First, he drew many small lines above an umbrella.

"Ah yes, rain! Yes, well, I suppose it does rain during the summer. A summer house would be a lovely place to use throughout the year."

The robot nodded as he continued scribbling, next drawing several things that didn't make much sense to Robert. There was an artist's painting easel, a piano, a violin, a harp, a birdhouse, and what looked like a figure of a girl.

"Okay, UMA, now I'm really confused!"

UMA rolled his eyes upwards in a gesture of frustration because Robert didn't understand. He sat, arms folded, tapping his scribblings and pointing up to the attic window.

"I get it, UMA. You want to build the summer house and put it on the Baccinos' roof? Is that it, pal?" asked Robert as the little robot put his shaking head in his hands, his whirling mechanical parts sounding like a groan.

A friendly old hand landed on UMA's shoulder. It was Dennis, who was smiling as he looked down at the robot's scribblings. "I understand, UMA," said the old man as he turned his head to look up at the attic window. "I see what you are trying to do, and I will help you. When I was a boy in Italy, we would always go bird-watching in the forest. The birds would only come close if we brought some bait."

The little robot nodded at Mr Baccino as his heart light bloomed a vibrant red glow, and he quickly clapped his hands to make a metal clinking sound.

It was then Robert's turn to wear a perplexed expression. "Hunting in Italy? Bait? What are you two talking about?" He felt out the loop and looked at his friends in annoyance.

UMA and Dennis looked back at him, both of them looking almost jubilant and nodding with whatever idea they were planning. Dennis patted UMA on the top of his round metal head, the robot's yellow eyes swelling with luminous golden warmth as he purred like a happy cat.

"Clever boy, UMA. Bright boy. This summer house – that's the bait. The angel bait."

Robert still didn't understand what the old Italian man was talking about. UMA joined Robert and stood next to him in the garden as they both looked up at the attic window, perched at the top of the old house. Robert was quite confused, *was that someone at the window?*, yet somehow suspected that the little robot was giggling deep inside his metal case.

11
Letting Go

Project Angel Bait started immediately and continued over the next few weeks of the summer holidays. Progress was swift and was helped by UMA working throughout the night. Sometimes Robert would be awoken in the middle of the night, and he would look out from his bedroom window and peer down into his neighbour's garden. He could usually make out UMA working under a dim lantern glow. The little robot seemed happy in his work, and his red circular chest light shone brightly as he worked on the summer house. He seemed very excited to create something special.

During the day, Robert was continually amazed at how many different tools popped out from UMA's body. Several of his fingers concealed tools that came in very useful: a drill, a screwdriver, a torch, spanners, paint brushes, etc. Robert thought back to the news video of all the robots that looked just like UMA, working in the Chinese car factory. No wonder the Chinese factories could make cars so quickly and much cheaper than any other countries. Robots did not get paid like ordinary human workers and robots like UMA never needed sleep.

The summer house was almost complete, and it already looked amazing. Lilly had made a few changes to the design and was very excited as it took shape in the idyllic garden. Dennis resisted the temptation to interfere too much and greatly admired how Robert and UMA had created something so beautiful. The old man was busy formulating the Angel Bait plan and was busy writing in his old notebook as his wife sat next to him, busily knitting a tartan blanket with the sounds of bustling workers coming from inside the summer house.

The music from the gramophone played in the background as Robert and UMA stepped out, looking proud and happy with themselves. "That's it, Mr and Mrs Baccino! I think we are all done! We made a few of the design changes you requested and the summer house is now open for business."

Dennis and Lilly looked at each other and applauded with a childlike excitement. Dennis stood and embraced Robert and UMA. "Wonderful work, boys. Excellent stuff! We cannot thank you enough. We are so grateful. We will never forget this."

UMA placed both of his small metal hands over his heart light as it shone a bright red. He could not hide how proud he was in helping his friendly old neighbours.

"I never quite figured out why we called it Project Angel Bait, though," Robert said, "but I am very proud of what we have built. Want to take a look inside and take the grand tour?" He was excited about showing off what they had created inside the summer house.

Dennis smiled and put his arm around Robert before leaning closer to him and whispering casually, "Angel bait tomorrow morning, my darling boy. You'll see."

***

The sun shone through the attic windows and cast shadows on the blank white walls. Velia Rose awoke in her bed and slowly opened her eyes to another new day. The room felt and sounded different as she sat up from her bed and looked around her attic room.

The drawings and paintings on her walls were all gone. In fact, everything was gone. The paints, pencils, charcoals, sketchbooks. The only things that remained in the room were a photo of her parents, and the six postcards she had received from them, still pinned on the wall. Velia Rose sat upright, in complete shock. Her small private world had disappeared. Her bedroom was like a blank canvas once again, and already she missed the colour that she had been bringing to the room.

Her grandparents stood together at the bedroom doorway. They held each other's hand and smiled, even though they looked unsure. They stood in the only doorway Velia Rose had used for the last few years to get to the nearby toilet and shower room. Other than that, she had remained in her attic room as a voluntary prisoner. Her grandparents approached the bed she sat on as she huddled her trembling legs under the cotton sheets.

Her grandfather spoke as his kind eyes twinkled in the morning light. "It's all okay, Velia Rose. Be calm, my darling. I know what you are probably thinking, and the answer is no, we have not been burgled."

He paused with a smile, hoping for a response, which eventually came in the form of puzzled look. Velia Rose felt afraid, and her eyes welled up as she realised the world she had built around her had now disappeared.

"It's time, my darling," her grandfather continued, stopping as he looked at the corner of the wall that held the photo and the postcards. "It's time to let go now. It's time to move on with your young life. Let us help you. We love you so much."

Velia Rose stepped on to the floorboards and raced to the corner, as if to hug the memories of her absent parents. She unpinned the photo and held it tight in her hand while she took one last glance at the postcards she must have read a hundred times over. She left the postcards pinned to the wall as she then turned and ran to her attic window, the place she had always felt secure. Her grandparents gently approached her, and they all looked down into the garden.

Over the last few weeks, Velia Rose had heard a lot of work going on below, and the busy sounds carried on well into the night. All the activity seemed to be down by the garden decking that sat perched on the canal, in an area of the garden that was concealed from her view by some small trees and conifers. Velia Rose had watched the boy and the robot come and go each day, but did not know what occupied them during the long hot summer days.

Dennis and Lilly slowly led Velia Rose down the stairs in the tall house. She could hear her grandfather's breathing get heavier, which in some way diverted the fear that pounded away in her chest as they reached the ground floor and made their way to the kitchen door that opened out to the garden. The back door was open, and the bright morning sunlight projected a haze over the kitchen's terracotta floor tiles. The aroma of strong Italian coffee and freshly baked bread filled Velia Rose with a gentle warm feeling. A maroon butterfly fluttered around the open doorway, moving in and out of the house until it returned to the garden and its many sweet flowers.

Velia Rose slowly slipped from her grandparent's grasp and stood still, locked rigidly in her pale blue pyjamas, staring at the sunlight pouring through the open door. She heard birdsong as she slowly stepped from the kitchen and out into the garden. The cool morning air was filled with floral scents. Lilly and Dennis closely followed Velia Rose outside as they both looked tentatively at each other with arched eyebrows.

Velia Rose moved slowly down the garden path and made her way to the small trees and conifers that stood at the end of the garden. She slowed as she reached them and turned her head as the sun sparkled a reflection from a circular window. She shielded her eyes from the sunlight and then opened them again to see a beautiful summer house, sitting proudly, close to the banks of the canal. It was a circular building with a coned roof. The summer house was made from beautiful maple wood, which had been expertly joined and varnished to make it look very natural and strong, like the hull of the greatest yacht. She knew that whoever had made the summer house had made it with expert craftsmanship and with a caring dedication. She walked around the circular building to find a raised wooden veranda surrounding an arched oak front door that faced out on to the gentle passing waters. Above the door was a sign, expertly carved on mahogany wood, which simply read "The Artist's Studio".

On one side of the doorway was a hanging bench, gently swaying in the breeze with warm-coloured blankets neatly stacked on the cushioned seat. On the other side stood a painter's easel, which faced the canal at the end of the garden. Velia Rose climbed the steps on to the veranda and opened the door to the summer house. She stepped inside, her eyes and mouth held wide open.

The wall, for it was just one large circular wall that surrounded the room, was covered in her drawings and paintings that had previously been in the attic room. The bright, vibrant colours she had created now lit up the room where she stood. The large room had at least six windows, and each window seemed to be precisely placed to provide a beautiful view of various colourful flowers, the fountain with its revolving statue, and the calm canal. She looked around the room, tears now trickling down her face as she saw her paints, pencils, papers, and charcoals lying on the most comfortable-looking bed. An upright piano stood by a harp, and looking through the harp strings, Velia Rose recognised the rounded curves of both a violin and an acoustic guitar. There was a small round table with three chairs scattered around it, a fresh jug of iced lemon water and a small bowl of fresh strawberries resting on its surface.

Velia Rose felt lightheaded and overwhelmed. Everything was just so perfect. She turned to see her grandparents standing behind her in the doorway, both still anxiously smiling at her. They slowly moved aside to reveal two more figures stood at the bottom of the stairs leading up to the veranda. It was the boy and the robot, both of them looking nervous. The little robot stood uneasy, tightly clutching a small bunch of red carnations that he had picked from the garden. Robert was enchanted and intrigued by the new visitor to the garden, for she was the most beautiful thing he had ever seen in his young life. He could also see that she looked incredibly pale, fragile, and delicate.

A relieved Dennis looked across to Robert and UMA, his breathing still heavy and his eyes glistening and coated with forming tears. "I think we have ourselves an angel. We can't thank you enough, boys. You do not know what you have done for us."

Velia Rose smiled and then laughed for the first time in many years. She ran to her grandparents and wrapped her arms around both of them. She didn't notice that she had just let go of the photo of her parents. She peeked between her grandparents, who were holding her tight, and could see the boy returning a warm, welcoming smile, while the little robot slowly edged towards her hesitantly with the prettiest bunch of red flowers she had ever seen.

Worlds wealthiest man still missing

By LIU MIN

The worlds wealthiest man, Champu Yamanuchi, is still missing. The 70 year old founder of Yamanuchi Robotics has now been missing for over 1 year and the Chinese police have made no progress in finding him. Mr Yamanuchi worked alone in his robotics lab and was thought to be working on AE (Artificial Emotion). He was known to be a keen sailor and fisherman, and police have been searching local waters with no success. The Yamanuchi Research Lab has now been closed. We have been unable to trace any family members.

st:
in
co
fig
re
ur
in
Ui
m.

he
tic
be
on
m
Ui
ve
to
ag
co
Tl
he
th
m
pa
ex
of
m
to
ex

13
The End of Summer

That summer was the happiest time of Robert's life. It wasn't just because he had met an incredible robot. It wasn't just because he was intrigued by a mysterious and gifted girl. It was the happiest time because he made the best friendships that his young life could recall. Throughout the remaining summer holidays, both he and UMA continued to work in the Baccinos' garden every day, but now they had a new friend – Velia Rose.

It didn't bother Robert that his best two friends did not speak. They all seemed to have a natural understanding of each other. Each day, Robert and UMA would work in the garden while Velia Rose would stand at her easel and draw or paint. Her work was becoming more colourful, as a sunny flush returned to her olive-skinned face. Dennis would tell them amazing, funny stories while they worked, and in the early afternoon, Lilly would serve a delicious lunch. Lilly seemed happiest of all. She was happy just to be surrounded by happy people, and most days they would enjoy a playful dance in the afternoon sun.

Velia Rose's most favourite part of the day was when they started to play music together. She had discovered she had a natural intuition for music and found it quite instinctive to pick up any instrument and help it to sing its own voice. While she still did not speak, she discovered that making music could help her express her emotions. Sometimes happy, sometimes sad, but always beautiful, moving music. Her favourite time was when she was playing the violin while UMA played the harp, and Robert would take a seat at the upright piano and do his best to follow. Dennis did not play any instrument, so he just had the sheer joy of sitting back in his reclining barber's chair. It was so relaxing at the canal edge on those sunny nights with the music playing from the open summer house. It was blissful for everyone that summer, and all of them felt like an accidental, slightly unusual, happy family.

UMA was still busy all the time. He still used Robert's laptop every day to search the Chinese Internet and was always looking at various maps. He also learned to become an excellent harpist and found that his small metal hands were very well suited to playing that instrument. The sounds of the harp vibrated on his metal-cased body when the harp rested against him as he played. He spent his nights watching videos about Makaton, a type of sign language he thought could help improve communication between both Velia Rose and himself. UMA could now remember over 500 Makaton signs, but the hard part would be teaching the signs to Velia Rose, Dennis and Lilly, and especially Robert.

UMA now felt at ease, and although he missed home, he treasured every new day as a gift of life. His heart light continued to shine its bright red light, and Robert realised that the light shone brightest when everyone spent time together.

Every night, once the sun went down and evening came to the garden, the small lighthouse that sat on top of the summer house would start shining its beam into the night sky. The pale yellow light beam would silently revolve around the garden and far into the distance, whenever it shone out through the garden opening that touched the canal-side. Robert often caught UMA either staring at the lighthouse beam, or at the small fisherman statue that also looked out into the night as it revolved atop the garden fountain. Robert wondered what they could be searching for. Velia Rose thought the same thing, but as always, kept the thought to herself.

During those summer months, Robert saw very little of his parents. Whenever he spent time with them, they seemed too distracted to notice him. They certainly didn't appear to enjoy being with him. Dennis had shared an old saying with Robert and UMA. "Attention is the rarest and purest form of generosity." Robert thought about that phrase while he sat in a restaurant with his parents, both of them distracted and busy on their mobile devices. He was becoming increasingly aware that more and more people chose to ignore each other and preferred to devour information from their personal devices.

Robert spent most of his time in the garden. It was a place that didn't feature any distracting technology other than his small and charming robot friend. UMA seemed most content being part of the new family in the garden, always looking to help others with no expectation of any reward. It seemed to Robert that UMA was just so happy to *belong* somewhere.

Robert and Velia Rose liked each other, although neither of them made that clear to anyone, most of all to each other. Most of the time, they were very happy playing in the garden like young childhood friends, but both of them sensed that the other person was unique. Velia Rose intrigued Robert. She was like a complex jigsaw puzzle that he felt compelled to complete if he had any hope of really knowing her. Each day, he would look at her drawings and paintings, and each day he would tell her that her work was amazing. What he really wanted to say to her was that *she* was amazing, but he somehow couldn't find the right moment.

Velia Rose felt very comfortable around Robert and just felt happier when he was close, which she didn't quite understand. He was a good-looking boy, but most of all, he was kind and honest. She felt she could trust and depend on him.

It was close to the end of the summer holidays, and all of them sat on the veranda of the summer house as the old gramophone played and the lighthouse shone out into the evening sky. Lilly had just cleared up after a delicious cannelloni supper, and they were now all cupping warm mugs of dark cocoa in the night chill. Dennis and Lilly enjoyed a slow dance on the garden lawn while UMA sat between Robert and Velia Rose on the hanging bench, swaying on the veranda of the summer house. Robert talked out loud into the night, knowing neither of his two companions would answer him back.

"It has been the greatest summer ever," he said as he looked up at the stars. "I don't want it to end, I wish we could stay like this forever."

UMA placed one metal hand on Robert's hand, and his other metal hand on Velia Rose's. Robert looked across at the three of them, all somehow connected and joined on the swaying bench. Velia Rose smiled, leant across, and kissed the robot's round metal head, prompting his heart light to bloom in the twilight.

Robert smiled and added, "Well, I'm certainly not kissing you, UMA! But I will give you this – you are such a brilliant robot. You saved me. Thanks, UMA."

Velia Rose stood up quickly and wagged her finger at Robert as if to correct whatever he had just said. This surprised Robert, as she usually stayed quiet and passive. He felt the need to defend himself and added, "But he *is* a clever robot, he brought us all together!"

Velia Rose once again wagged her finger at Robert as UMA sat silently, quietly observing the girl.

She stepped across to her drawing equipment and reached for a pencil and her sketchpad. She flicked through the pages until she found a blank page and furiously began scribbling and scratching at the paper with her drawing pencil. After a few moments, she stopped and turned to show the sketchpad to Robert and UMA. Her picture featured two different figures standing side by side. The first figure was a realistic portrayal of UMA, but over the little robot's head Velia Rose had crayoned a large red X. Next to UMA, was a drawing of a man – the figure had no facial features. Above the picture of the man, Velia Rose had crayoned a large green tick.

Robert paused for a moment and looked up at Velia Rose before nodding and quietly adding, "I understand. I understand, and I agree with you, Velia Rose. UMA is more like a person than a robot."

Velia Rose nodded and sighed quietly with relief, while the little robot dropped his head as if embarrassed. This time, Robert stood up and stepped towards the artist's easel that was standing on the veranda. He flipped open the paint box, rummaged around, and soon returned to the robot with a small paintbrush in his hand. The robot remained seated and eyed Robert suspiciously as the boy knelt before him.

"Now keep still, my friend, this won't hurt one bit," Robert whispered as he raised the brush, which glistened with red paint. He slowly and carefully painted a red letter on the robot's chest. He was just about to paint another letter when Velia Rose joined him and tenderly took the paintbrush from his hand as she smiled. She somehow understood what Robert was thinking and continued the work by painting another red letter on to the robot's chest.

The pair of them stood hand in hand before the little robot, both now looking down at him sitting on the hanging bench. UMA lowered his head to read the letters that were now inscribed on his metal-cased chest. His eyes shone a bright yellow while his heart light throbbed a deep red glow. His small metal hands seem to cup his heart light, maybe to contain his emotions. He could not take his eyes away from his new inscription. It was like he had received a tattoo that he would be proud to wear for the rest of his life.

The robot looked up to see his friends, Robert and Velia Rose, smile with genuine happiness. He looked down again, his little feet quickly tapping on the veranda in giddy excitement. He now felt very different and had a warm sense of acceptance. He would never tire of reading it; it made him feel wanted.

UMA hovered his metal fingers over the freshly painted letters and read it over and over again...

THE LONELIEST ROBOT
Part 2

(Five years later)

14
Five Years Older

The little robot sat alone on the see-saw in the garden. From the lower end, he gazed into the empty space of the up-ended see-saw, tilted into the twilight sky. He looked down at his chest, tracing his metal fingers over the painted letters, noticing that the edges were now slightly chipped and the surface of the red paint was starting to crack. However, after five years, he could still easily read hUMAn, and this never failed to make him feel very proud.

The last five years had represented a wonderfully splendid time for everyone who shared the joys of the Baccinos' garden. Of course, the sun did not shine every day, and there had been times when everyone was not entirely delighted with life. During these times, everyone came together to help try to fix things and make them better again.

Dennis and Lilly Baccino were now five years older, and like many older people, they had slowed down quite a lot. Instead of dancing in the garden, they stayed close and held each other's hands as they listened to the old gramophone that played the familiar music. Every day, they still sat on the bank of the canal and cheerfully waved at the passing barges, and most of all, they enjoyed watching Velia Rose grow into a beautiful and polite seventeen-year-old young lady.

Robert and UMA were still regular visitors to the garden, and the Baccinos regarded them as "our two boys", and treated them as if they were two sons. Dennis and Lilly felt very proud of Velia Rose, Robert, and UMA. Dennis now used a walking stick to help him get around the garden, and Velia Rose had learned how to cook from Lilly and had now taken over most of the duties in the kitchen (although Lilly still insisted in making her special Italian pasta sauces from her secret recipes.)

The garden had been further transformed, and over the years it had flourished into an idyllic paradise, a delightful wonderland for all of them to enjoy. The garden had won several awards in *The*

Gardener Monthly magazine, and some people had even asked the Baccinos to consider opening the garden to the public. Of course, the Baccinos were very flattered, but they declined the option as they valued privacy and family time so much.

Robert and UMA had designed the garden to a very detailed level so that each week, a new beautiful flower would come into bloom. There was always a splash of floral colour in the garden, even during the cold winter months. The garden included a small playground which Robert, Velia Rose, and UMA had enjoyed when they were younger, but now it seemed that it was just UMA who played on the swing, the slide, and the see-saw.

Velia Rose and Robert had also designed and constructed an aviary, and this provided a home to many beautiful birds without caging them in a small confined space. The birds in the aviary would play, fly, and sing to each other and this brought more life to the garden. Every day, UMA would open the aviary's ornate wire doors to allow any birds to leave if they wished to, but as they were happy in the garden, they always chose to stay in the aviary. Quite often a few of the small bluebirds would fly to UMA, resting on his shoulder or arm before tweeting and chirping away. UMA's favourite bird in the aviary was a great cormorant which Robert had nicknamed "Shadow". He called him Shadow because the great cormorant liked to follow UMA all around the garden closely. Shadow was a large bird with dark feathers and a yellow hooked bill, and it enjoyed waddling behind the robot as he worked in the garden. Robert had read somewhere that this type of bird was traditionally used to help Chinese fishermen catch fish.

The summer house still looked splendid, and as Velia Rose now lived in it, it included heating and a small kitchen. She didn't care much for television as it mostly involved desperate celebrities, but she enjoyed watching some movies and would most often spend her nights painting, listening to music, or reading books. All of the wall space in the summer house was now covered in her colour pictures, and she still had the old photo of her parents pinned to the wall even though she had not heard anything from them since she was a young girl.

Over the years, UMA had taught Velia Rose to use the Makaton sign language, and this allowed her to communicate with everyone in the garden. While this helped matters, Lilly was still convinced that Velia Rose chose not to use her inner voice for a reason she could not understand, and she prayed every single night that one day Velia Rose would find her voice.

Velia Rose was beautiful, with dark flowing black hair that surrounded her elegant and lovely face. Her eyes, large and rounded, were dark brown and resembled warm and sweet dark chocolate. She had grown to be a capable and confident young lady and had already created her own website to sell her art. She would communicate by email with her customers and was rather hopeful that she could be a professional artist when she was older.

Robert, UMA, and Velia Rose had even written and recorded some beautiful music that the website would play while people browsed through her drawings and paintings. It seemed to be working, as she had received customer orders from all around the world. She did not go to school and had learned much from her grandparents or from following specific educational lessons on the Internet. The only people that she really knew in the world were the people in her small garden. She was frightened about leaving the garden, as many images she had watched on the television news made her feel that the world was a cold and dangerous place. Velia Rose had grown especially close to Robert, and while they were not exactly boyfriend and girlfriend, they trusted each other and seemed to understand what the other was thinking. She loved him but did not want to scare him away if she ever declared her love to him, especially as Robert seemed to be changing over the last year or so . . .

***

Robert entered the garden through the gate in the hedges, his head hovering over his mobile device as he walked to the canal deck to join Dennis and Lilly Baccino, who were already sitting at the table, taking afternoon tea with jam and cream scones.

Robert was distracted on his mobile device and seemed quite irritated. "This thing is so slow, it's impossible to do anything with it!" he snapped, before lobbing the mobile device on to the oak table, where it landed by the red teapot.

"I badly need to upgrade, get a Megafasti-Mobi like my dad's."

Dennis and Lilly looked at each other before Robert added with frustration, "I mean, how is it not possible to watch three movies while videoconferencing into my lessons. That thing sucks!"

Dennis broke the silence by asking, "But you can still do a lot with that device? Eh, Robert? It still works okay? No?"

Robert looked frustrated and snapped, "It still works, but it can't do many things at the same time, it's just not powerful enough! Everyone in college has got better ones."

Dennis nodded as he looked out at the quiet canal. The wise old Italian paused before turning back to Robert to say, "I think it was Theodore Roosevelt who once said, 'Comparison is the thief of all joy'."

Robert shook his head as the old man continued, "Sometimes we are all guilty of looking at others who have something we don't have. Be yourself, Robert – if you try to be like others, then you will only become someone else, and that person won't be your real self. Always respect others, but try to resist any comparison. No good can come from it."

Robert remained still with his gaze locked down on the mobile device. "You don't understand, Mr Baccino. I can't do all the stuff I need to do with that old thing on the table. It's prehistoric!"

"Like us?" joked the old man.

"I didn't mean it that way. It's just annoying that everyone else can do whatever they want, and do it in milliseconds, while I have to wait and wait. Sometimes for a full minute! It's stressful, man, and it's bumming me out!" Robert reached over and grabbed at the few remaining biscuits from the plate on the table.

Dennis and Lilly exchanged a brief glance between them before Mr Baccino decided to change the subject in an attempt to lighten the mood. "We had a good laugh earlier on, Robert. Little UMA was being followed by Shadow again, but guess what? Shadow must be a new dad cos he had eight young little chicks shadowing him this time. It looked like UMA was leading a conga dance! All ten of them in a line!" The old couple giggled at the recent memory as Robert kept his eyes fixed on his mobile device, which sat next to the teapot.

"You should have seen it, Robert! Even Velia Rose was pointing and giggling at them! I hope she draws or paints that scene, what a picture that one would be."

Roberts' mind seemed elsewhere, and after a moment, Dennis asked, with concern in his voice, "You okay, Robert? What's on your mind, son?"

Robert paused for a moment and eventually gave a decisive nod of the head as he said emphatically, "Yeah, definitely going to go for a Megafasti-Mobi model with 2 million megs."

The Baccinos did not know what to say as a new and awkward silence filled the garden.

***

UMA returned to the garden later that afternoon. After feeding the birds in the aviary and cleaning the windows of the summer house, the little robot sat down at the laptop for his daily one-hour laptop session. He would usually browse Google Maps and was hopeful more and more images would be released or updated so he could view more satellite images of China. The robot scanned various Chinese websites and after an hour, gently lowered the lid of the laptop until it clicked into the closed position. He looked up at the revolving fountain statue as his heart light slowly pulsed with a dull blue light.

Over the last five years, UMA had extended his help beyond the Baccinos' garden and was now helping people in the local hospital, which did not have much money. He helped out at some local schools and also volunteered at local old people's homes, and each week he would take the old folk out on river cruises. UMA couldn't understand why old people stayed locked inside these types of places. Everyone he took on the river cruise rides always smiled, laughed, and enjoyed the day.

One thing that UMA had learned to understand was what brightened the day of the older people. He learned that the old faces would always light up whenever he brought young children from the local schools to visit them. He could see the delight in the eyes of the older people, talking and smiling as if the presence of the children were recharging their old bones with a renewed love and energy for life. Most of the time, the children did not realise what joy they brought to other people, just by giving them some time and attention. Even several hours after each children's visit had ended, the older people would laugh and talk about the wonderful, beautiful children. UMA realised that older people somehow needed younger people. It stopped them feeling lonely and made them feel alive. UMA still missed his father and wished he could see him again, but his hope had almost entirely faded over the last five years.

Rather than dwell on the pain of losing his father, UMA just wanted to help others and bring people together. The little robot had learned that you had to look forward with hope, rather than look back with any regrets.

15
Commercial Break

Robert Karma sat alone in his bedroom, his face illuminated as he sat at his games console, hypnotically staring at the large TV screen on his bedroom wall. He was wearing a large combat-style headset that allowed him to talk to the other online gamers who were also playing "Attack Force 5 – The Redemption", the new number one computer game release that required teams to find and destroy the enemy. Extra points were available if you could kidnap and terrify some innocent hostages.

Robert wasn't sure if he really enjoyed playing the game, but he was increasingly enjoying the comfort of seclusion from other people. When he was playing games with his headset at full blast, he didn't have to talk or deal with real people or even UMA. He could disappear into the virtual world of his games and escape from real life for hours, sometimes for most of the day. His mum and dad didn't seem to mind. They were too busy wasting their own time to worry if Robert was spending more and more time submerged in his private universe. Playing games was easier than doing the gardening work in the Baccinos' garden. Besides, UMA was mostly out and about doing other things, and Velia Rose was busy doing more housework and cooking to help her grandmother. Robert was starting to feel a bit detached from everyone.

He had started to feel a strong compulsion to show that he could be successful. He wanted to prove to his dad that he could also be important. He *needed* to show his mother that he wasn't an idiot. He wanted to taste life outside the Baccino garden and outside school. Life seemed too simple just now. His parents seemed happiest (for at least a few days) whenever they bought something new. Robert wanted to find success, even if it meant losing some things, or someone. His father had told him many times, "Anything worth having in life is something you have to work hard for. You must give *everything*."

All the online games that Robert played now featured two-minute adverts, which would appear once he destroyed 100 enemies. He realised he had been playing the game for almost six hours and quickly estimated that he must have watched over 150 commercials during this particular gaming session. Most of the adverts featured smiley pretty people buying new stuff to make them happier. *Those advert people seem to have it all,* thought Robert. They *could* have it all, getting more and more stuff to make them happier, having a brilliant life, usually just for an incredibly low-cost, affordable monthly payment. Robert stared at the TV adverts and wondered if he could ever be as happy as the smiley pretty people on them. Every time he used social media, he would see a continual stream of other people having incredible fun somewhere else around the world. Usually, they were wearing designer clothes, eating in the best places, and having it all, while Robert just sat alone in his bedroom playing on his games console. He wanted an awesome, exciting life as well.

He didn't enjoy college, and the very thought of more education time at some university didn't appeal to him. He wanted to see more of the world, and he was starting to feel trapped in his small hometown. He didn't know what he wanted to be once he was older, but he was sure about what he didn't want – he didn't want to be just another average person, living an ordinary life, in his average hometown. His dad had recently shown him his latest salary payslip, which included a big bonus payment for terminating twenty jobs, allowing the company to make more profit. Robert couldn't believe how much money he could make if he became a successful businessman just like his dad. Just imagine all the stuff you could buy with that much money!

He frowned and felt a ball of frustration build in his belly as the next advert glared from the bright TV screen. This advert featured a large group of pretty young people partying on a beach. Everyone was smiling, and the boys and girls laughed and danced as they were served delicious food and drink, while the crazy-looking DJ made them all laugh as he rolled around on the white sands of the beach as he yelled out "Woop! Woop! Mega Woop!" It looked like a fun, crazy party, and everyone looked so perfect and happy. Then a beautiful woman appeared on the screen while the party continued on the beach behind her. She was smiling and dancing as she looked out from the TV screen. She wore a red bikini, which had a large badge pinned to it, and the badge read "Debbie, VP of Recruitment."

"Every day at DiaboliCo is a cool, fun day! Join us and make your dreams a reality! We are now recruiting and looking for exciting fresh talent just like you." The lady presenter pointed right at Robert from the TV screen and quickly spun around, shaking her glossy blonde hair and flashing her perfect bright white teeth, before continuing.

"Let us be a part of you! We can transform you! Don't worry, we understand, we *get you*! Do you want to be a somebody, or a nobody? Do you want a successful life? You got it with DiaboliCo! Apply today. You won't regret it. Free mobile handset for all applications made today!"

Small blurry words, far too small and fast-moving, scrolled along the bottom of the screen as the group on the beach all danced by some palm trees before a beautiful sunset on the horizon of the ocean. The only words that Robert recognised on the fast-moving text were "Disclaimer" and "Apply today!" All the other words seemed to pass by in a blur. It didn't matter anyway; his mind was already made up. He wanted to be successful and have an incredible life. He wanted to join DiaboliCo. Whoever they were, wherever they were based, and whatever they did. At that moment, DiaboliCo had all the answers to the questions in Robert's mind. He just wanted someone who understood him. Someone who could *get him*.

He then dropped his game controller and quickly tapped in the Internet address to make his job application. In less than seven minutes, he had completed the application form, allowing him more time to return to his private world of Attack Force 5 – The Redemption. If he could just finish this level of the game, then he could then watch a few movies alone in his room.

Velia Rose stood alone in the garden and looked up at the attic window. She often thought about the years she had spent watching the world from the other side of the glass, which now reflected the late afternoon sun. It seemed a different world to her now. She was a busy girl, and life seemed splendid in most ways. She loved living in the garden summer house, and she had made it even more comfortable over the last few years. Most days she still wanted to draw and paint and she had even managed to set up her website to share her work and sell some of her artwork.

UMA was a great help to her, as she still didn't feel brave enough to leave the safety of the Baccino garden, so whenever she needed anything, or if she needed to mail some of her artwork to a customer, then the little robot would happily oblige. UMA had worked very hard and patiently to teach Velia Rose how to use Makaton, the sign language she used for communication with others in the garden. She could now remember at least 500 signs and could communicate quite well, especially with UMA. She also loved to play music as much as her art and practised both the piano and violin every day.

When she wasn't playing music, she would listen to music in the summer house, and she found it easy to get lost in it – it comforted her. More recently, however, she had noticed that her free time was becoming less as she had to help her grandparents around the house. She worried about them both as they were getting older and a bit slower. They still radiated a warm, pure happiness that she treasured, but Velia Rose knew life would not get easier for them, even if she and UMA did much of the work around the house and garden. She no longer thought about her absent parents. She couldn't find a way to feel about them, so decided the best way to deal with them was to try to put them out of her mind.

What worried Velia Rose most, though, was that she was seeing less and less of her special friend, Robert. She didn't understand why he no longer came around every day. He now visited just a few times a week. Velia Rose could sense he was eager to find his own path in life and find himself in some way. He looked a little bit lost to her, but as she did not speak, she found it difficult to understand why he felt this way. She could tell that UMA was also worried about Robert. Every day, the little robot would walk between the hedges of the nearby gardens and go looking for him.

Lately, Robert had chosen to stay at home most days. Velia Rose thought she had done something wrong, as they had always been such good friends. Her grandmother had tried to explain that people sometimes change in life, and sometimes friends can come and go. But Velia Rose didn't want to believe this. Her world revolved around the beautiful garden, her grandparents, the little robot, and the boy who lived next door. Her chest felt an empty pain whenever she thought of Robert.

She looked up at the attic window again. How she regretted spending so much time alone in that small room at the top of the house, watching the world spin by. Now her best friend, who lived just next door was choosing to be alone, his preferred companions being his mobile phone, computer, game console, and TV. She didn't understand it.

People needed people.

16
Separation

Robert sat alone in his room, busy scrolling down the screen of his mobile device. He had been watching animal videos, which were supposed to be hilarious, but he hadn't even raised a smile as he finished watching a video of a baby pig riding on a skateboard. He didn't even think as he automatically selected another stupid clip. The next mind-numbing video of a dancing chicken was about to start as Robert noticed a new mail notification alert flash on his mobile device. He opened the email and saw a new mail from debbie_de_ceiver@diabolico.com, and the email was flashing its title in a bright blue text – "Welcome to DiaboliCo! We really get you!"

Robert quickly opened the email and scanned its contents. He was delighted to find it was a formal job offer from DiaboliCo. His job start date was just two days away, and he was instructed to report to the company headquarters office in the city. On arrival at DiaboliCo Towers at 5:30 a.m., he should ask for Debbie DeCeiver, the Vice President of recruitment.

Robert was a little surprised that he had landed the new position so quickly, as the video interview he'd done had felt embarrassing as he didn't have any real academic qualifications or job experience to share. However, it had gone very well once he'd told them that he was willing to do absolutely anything to succeed at DiaboliCo and was prepared to give his everything to help the company succeed. They were delighted to hear that he liked technology and had no health issues. The job offer e-mail explained that all he had to do was promptly sign the attached employment contract and return it to DiaboliCo within seven minutes. This condition didn't allow Robert enough time to read, or even understand, the accompanying 208-page employment contract. However, he felt sure they must be a very credible and trustworthy company, so he went ahead and signed the document and then clicked an icon button within the

76

email which read ACCEPT ASSIGNMENT before the seven-minute deadline expired.

Robert raced downstairs to share the exciting news with his parents. He entered the lounge and wasn't entirely surprised to see his mother sprawled on the large leather couch with her feet resting upon a footstool. At her feet stood UMA, dutifully providing a gentle foot massage. Consooma Karma lay back on the couch with her face covered in thick yellow face cream and her eyes covered with large slices of ugly fruit. She had read that the essential oils and nutrients in the expensive skin lotion would revitalise her skin and make her look radiant and young again. Just now, though, she resembled a giant flabby blob with a snake's head. Her ugly fruit-covered eyes looked menacing as she muttered, "Ooh. Just there! That's it, Supa UMA, really squeeze the balls of my feet, they ache so much from all the walking down the stairs this morning. Ooh, yes, that's it, just there . . . lovely jubbly, UMA babes."

UMA continued with the foot massage but didn't look like he was enjoying the experience. The little robot grimaced at the ugly feet and looked up as Robert entered the room, his chest light morphing from a pale blue light to a bright red glow. Robert noticed his father was sitting in an armchair in the lounge, tapping out a new email on his laptop while he wore his telephone conference headset, occasionally muttering, "Agreed, Clive", "Crucial, Clive", and "Absolutely, Clive".

Robert gave a mild cough and then made his announcement to the lounge and its occupants. His parents and UMA all stopped and turned to face him. Consooma lifted a slice of ugly fruit from one of her puffy eyelids as she peeked at her son.

"I've got a new job, and I start in two days. I will be moving to the city. It's a great opportunity in a brilliant company called —" He was about to continue with his announcement but was interrupted by a high-pitched heckling laugh coming from his mother. She apparently thought it was hilarious.

She lifted her short stubby arms and pointed at her son. "You! Working? In the city? You are joking, right? Ha! The very thought of some pathetic loser like you working in a professional organisation! They must be desperate to take a chance on you. Although, can you get me some edible Hungarian dessertspoons from the city? They are all the rage on Mind Numb TV!"

Robert felt immediately deflated and searched the room, hoping to find a better reaction from his father, who was still busy on his conference call.

Keith Karma realised his son was looking across at him as he repeated, "Absolutely, Clive. Agreed, Clive. Crucial, Clive." He looked down at his headset control button and quickly pressed the microphone mute button, before hastily adding, "Er, well done, son. Can you be sure to empty your room and get rid of that robot before you go? Pretty sure his radio waves interfere with the mobile reception I get on my important calls. Good lad. Maybe see you at Christmas?"

Without waiting for an answer, he then un-muted his microphone and seamlessly returned to his conference call by adding a "Crucial, Clive, take that out of Clause 4c and put in back in Clause 4b. Well spotted, Clive."

UMA could feel Robert's pain as all of his father's attention was promptly consumed by work once again. The robot walked to Robert and gently took his hand, leading him out of the lounge and through to the back door of the house. Robert could still hear his mother's cackling laughter coming as UMA led him through the garden hedge and into the Baccino garden. Robert felt happy, sad, and angry at the same time. He wanted to prove to his parents that he could become successful; maybe then they would give him their attention, approval, or some loving support.

***

Velia Rose stood on the canal-side decking, her grandfather reclining beside her on his old barber's chair with his hands held behind his head and his feet tapping on the thick silver footrest. Her grandmother sat knitting in the large comfy armchair, surrounded by several soft cushions. The gramophone played its tinny low volume sound as UMA led Robert towards them. They all turned and gave a welcoming smile as Dennis Baccino raised his hand and waved at them,

"Ah, boys, my two boys! What a pleasant surprise! Are you joining us for lunch today, Robert? We were just about to have a cup of tea and listen to some new music Velia Rose has written."

Velia Rose lowered her head but still eyed Robert with a nervous smile as she gestured her hands to signal that it was a piano piece. Robert nodded and gave a small thumbs-up gesture to Velia Rose. He loved to hear her play the piano. She only ever played her own music, and it always sounded haunting but beautiful at the same time. She seemed delighted to have Robert and UMA back in the garden and quickly skipped across to the upright piano, which stood on the veranda of the summer house. She had painted the wooden piano case in many vibrant bright colours, and it looked like an exploding firework.

Dennis sat up in his old barber's chair and leant forward to lift the gramophone arm from the crackly old vinyl disc so that the garden was now almost silent, with just the distant chugging of a canal barge and the hushed quiet birdsong drifting from the aviary. His chair slowly swivelled and turned so that he, his wife Lilly, Robert, and UMA faced Velia Rose as she lowered herself on to the piano stool.

Velia Rose looked across at all the people she loved so much and produced a beaming yet humble smile before dropping her hands and head as she readied herself to share her new composition. She began to play, her eyes closed, and she was instantly lost as the music flowed from her through the piano, filling the garden with wonder. The music was very moving, and although it featured no words, it carried real emotion as if it poured from the young girl's heart.

The piano sounded its sad melody, which lifted with a powerful and hopeful chorus. The music continued to flow from her and mesmerised her grandparents, their proud faces now reflecting a gentle red bloom that came from the bright shining heart light of UMA. They all moved closer, her old grandparents taking small shuffling steps so all of them could gather around the piano as the music continued to swirl its magic around the garden. Velia Rose continued to play with her eyes closed and her body swaying as both of her hands caressed the piano keys. She was totally lost now, and it felt a great place to be, especially when others enjoyed the melancholic music she played. It was her way of talking to the world. After a hazy few minutes, she stopped playing as the final minor note faded its lonely sound.

Velia Rose slowly lifted her head and opened her wet eyes in what should have been a beautiful moment for all of them to share. That moment was lost, however, as it was rudely interrupted by an abrasive and annoying ringtone, which featured ugly bass sounds with repetitive electronic drums, coming from Robert's mobile phone.

Everyone looked at him, expecting him to be embarrassed and to silence the vibrating device quickly. However, Robert looked down and could see it was an incoming call from Debbie DeCeiver. He recognised the photo of Debbie, and he remembered her beautiful model-type looks from the recruitment advert he watched on the TV.

At that moment, Robert made his decision, and it explained to everyone where his attention so clearly was. He looked down at the "answer call" button as the phone continued to blare out its irritating muzak, before looking up and over the piano into Velia Rose's eyes. They looked deep into each other's eyes for just a few seconds, before Robert dropped his gaze, lowered his head, and turned away as he talked into the blue glowing mobile phone, now edging away from the summer house.

"Hi, Debbie! You have reached Robert Karma. I am so excited about coming to work for DiaboliCo! How may I assist you today?"

Velia Rose heard every word and closed her eyes again. This time she wasn't lost in her music, but lost in her pain. Dennis and Lilly Baccino looked at Velia Rose and then at each other, before taking each other's hand. UMA stood still and silent at the side of the piano, now feeling quite lost himself.

Robert continued his short discussion, before ending the call with, "Super-cool! Looking forward to day one! Just be sure that I will give *my everything* for DiaboliCo. See you soon, Debbie. Awesome. Bye."

Robert tapped the "end call" icon on the mobile phone as he looked up at his friends. It was more than an awkward silence that filled the air, and he edged back towards them again. Velia Rose remained sat at the piano with her eyes closed and her head held low.

Dennis was the first to talk. "You going away, son?" the old man asked.

Robert shrugged.

"You going to move away and get your own place in the city?" Robert nodded.

"This job, is it really what you want, son?"

Robert shrugged again and then nodded.

"You *will* still come and visit, won't you, boy? Welcome any time here, you know that, Robert. This place is always here for you."

Robert offered no response. He was already busy doing something else on his phone.

***

A few hours passed, and the darkness of twilight began to fill the sky. Robert had spent the last few hours making travel and accommodation arrangements for his move to the city. He arranged for a moving company to collect his boxed-up possessions and deliver them to his new one-person city apartment his employer would supply. He looked around his bedroom one last time. He could hear his mother in her nearby bedroom phoning through an order for something she had spotted on the shopping channel. He could hear movement above in the converted loft office and assumed his dad would be walking around the small space, babbling into his headset that was attached to his round, fat, bald, and empty head.

This room and house didn't hold great memories, Robert thought as he stepped towards the window. He peered down into the garden, and he could see the old garden shed, the place where he first discovered UMA in the middle of the night. He smiled faintly and looked across to the Baccino garden but could not see anyone. He could only see the revolving fisherman statue, peeking above the hedges that separated the two gardens, the lonely figure continually searching into the night as it slowly rotated.

Robert hated goodbyes, so he found it easier to slip quietly from the house while his parents were distracted with work and buying more stuff they didn't need. He was travelling light, as the moving company was transporting all his clothes and big stuff. All he had to carry was his mobile phone. He placed it in both hands as he traipsed along a path and out into the night. He was heading for the railway station where he would catch a train that would take him into the city. He peeked above his mobile device and could see the blue glow of the bustling city in the distance – the same blue glow that shone up on to his face from his mobile phone. The city towers stood high and imposing into the night sky. Robert looked at the city, the great place of opportunity where dreams could come true, before returning his gaze to his mobile phone. He had already started receiving work emails and wanted to respond to them as quickly as possible. As Robert tapped away on his mobile device, he heard a familiar gentle clinking sound from behind.

It was then that Robert turned and realised that UMA had been quietly following him. The little robot stood still with an old shabby suitcase quietly swaying in his nervous metallic grip. UMA stared at Robert in silence, his circular heart light slowly pulsing with a faint red glow. The light-glow quickly changed to a dull, cold blue glare as Robert stopped and shook his head. Robert then pointed back to The Baccino garden,

"Go back UMA. The garden is your home."

UMA shook his metallic head in silent disagreement.

"It's your home UMA. Go home! I need to go alone. I need to show people that I can do this. I can be a real success, but please, let me do this. Please...go home." Robert turned away and continued his lonely journey into the city.

***

UMA sat alone beneath an old apple tree that sat at the back of the Baccino garden. He watched Robert walking away into the night, his figure becoming smaller and smaller as he moved further away, silhouetted on the blue glowing orb of the city sphere. The little robot thought it resembled a big cold dome. UMA rested his hand on the old tin watering can and slowly tapped his metal fingers on its handle. His heart light pulsed with a blue glow and then pulsed with a red tinge. He had felt like this before, years before, when he was back in China. That was his real home. No-one understood how lost and far from home the little robot really was. UMA watched Robert disappear from view with the familiar feeling of losing someone and not knowing when – or if – you would ever see them again. It was happening again.

Right there, alone under the apple tree, sat a lonely robot.

17
Welcome to DiaboliCo

Robert stood before the high tower block that was the global headquarters of DiaboliCo. He looked up at the tall glass-fronted tower, which reached into the early morning sky. The superstructure was so big that he could not see the top of the building, which pierced the morning clouds above. He lowered his head and approached the tall and thick glass-doored entrance. A friendly looking security guard sat at a large marble desk in the reception area and noticed Robert through the glass door; the guard nodded and pressed a button which allowed the entrance doors to open slowly. A warm, inviting smell of fresh coffee and morning baked bread filled the reception air as Robert entered the building.

It was 5:20 a.m., and Robert was surprised to see people scuttling around the reception area and lining up to take one of eight elevators. The workers lined up in complete silence for each of the elevators, and as each one arrived, they filed dutifully into the large metal boxes. Each and every worker held a mobile device which seemed to absorb all of their attention while they moved around the building.

Robert approached the man seated behind the reception desk. He sat behind a large computer screen that looked very serious and professional, until Robert realised the man was watching a goofy video of a baby pig on a skateboard. Just as Robert was about to speak, the receptionist started a telephone conversation. It was clearly a private call, as the man smiled and lovingly touched a framed photograph of a pretty young girl that stood next to his desk telephone. Robert stood patiently and overheard some of the conversation, "...just wanted to wish you well at school today honey. Looking forward to seeing you tonight. We can both fix dinner up and I can help you with your homework before I start another night-shift...love you too..." The receptionist then became aware that Robert was waiting for assistance and quickly ended his private call.

"Hey, I saw that video clip too! It's so great man, so funny!" Robert said enthusiastically to the receptionist. The man slowly tilted his screen away from Robert's view and kept a stern face until suddenly a broad smile flickered into life on his face and his eyes widened. It was like someone had just flicked a switch to bring him to life.

"Good morning, sir, and welcome to DiaboliCo! How may I help you today?" the beaming receptionist asked.

"Good morning, my name is Robert Karma, and I'm here to start my new job. I have been instructed to ask for Debbie DeCeiver," Robert replied.

"Certainly, sir! I'll call Debbie straight away and inform her you are here. Please take a seat and enjoy complimentary coffee and pastries. Debbie will be right with you."

Robert thanked the receptionist and sat down on some plush leather sofas, feeling quite small on the couch, as it could comfortably seat eight people. He felt very comfortable already, even though it seemed odd that everyone quickly shuffled around in silence, head lowered, wearing serious expressions. He noticed several people wearing thick-rimmed glasses and assumed it was the current fashion in the big city. He was just about to leaf through some of the numerous magazines that lay on the table, all of them showing either an expensive sports cars or a beautiful face emblazoned on the front cover, when a croaky old voice sounded above him.

"Welcome to DiaboliCo. I'm Debbie DeCeiver. You must be Robert Karma. The new starter."

Robert looked up and sat surprised, his mouth agape. This Debbie was certainly not the Debbie that appeared on the recruitment advert. This lady had fuzzy red hair, freckles, and was very tall and impossibly skinny.

"I know, I know. Where is the foxy chick wearing the red bikini from the TV advert? Forget it, kid! They use actors for those adverts. The lady who plays me is a Russian fashion model. The boss said I would scare away any new recruits, so we have to use actors. Even for my phone photo!"

Debbie looked down at Robert. She had a sour-looking face which carried a pained expression, and Robert thought she looked like she had just drunk a large glass of malt vinegar.

She screwed up her face again as she said abruptly, "C'mon, get up. Follow me. Quick, now. You don't want to be late for the boss. He loves a reliable and efficient worker."

Robert ran after Debbie DeCeiver as she headed for an open

elevator to take them to level 162. She did not say anything as the elevator moved up inside DiaboliCo Tower but instead tutted and pursed her lips every time the elevator stopped at any intermittent floors. Eventually, they reached level 162, and they both stepped out from the elevator as four people entered the elevator, all of them wearing thick-rimmed spectacles and grim expressions. They stepped into a long corridor, which was covered in a thick blue carpet.

Debbie stood still and raised her long skinny arm to point her white bony finger down the long hallway. "That door at the end," she mumbled. "Office number one. Knock three times and wait for the green light above the door. You get a two-minute welcome with the boss and then head back down to level -19 to start work in your office. Here is your security badge. Work hard, fully comply, and you will do well around here, kid. Remember, stay in the green."

Robert was puzzled. "Stay in the green?"

Debbie was already back in the elevator, and as the doors began to close, she looked Robert up and down with a knowing half-smile before offering, "You'll figure it out." The four people standing behind Debbie in the elevator chuckled away to each other as the doors closed.

Robert stood alone in the corridor. He looked down at his plastic security badge that stated it must be displayed at all times. The pass held his photo he had submitted with his application form, his name, department and office location: Robert Karma, Internal Logistics, level -19.

More interestingly, above his photo were three small coloured circles. Each circle was the same size and arranged in a horizontal row, but each circle was a different colour. There was a red, amber, and green circle. He attached the security pass to his trouser belt, and the green circle started to flash a mild and pleasant green pulsing light. Robert thought it looked cool and quickly understood what Debbie had meant when she had said, "Stay in the green."

He looked up and walked down the quiet corridor towards the large ominous-looking door at the end. Just before he reached it, he passed an open office doorway and glanced across at an attractive blonde woman who was sitting at her desk and wholly preoccupied with pouting at her camera phone and looking for the perfect selfie to circulate to her friends on social media who she didn't really know. She darted a cold and unfriendly look at Robert as he passed her doorway and reached his destination. It was a large heavy door made from hard dark wood, with a carved wooden nameplate fixed to the centre of the door. On the nameplate, in bold letters, it read:

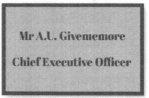

Mr A.U. Givememore

Chief Executive Officer

Above the door were three lights, each one shaded in a different colour. Again, the colours were red, amber, and green. As instructed, Robert knocked three times on the cold, hard wood and looked up to see if the green light would signal him to enter. Instead, the central amber light flashed as Robert heard a raised voice coming from the other side of the solid office door. The voice sounded deep and authoritative and sounded like it was issuing a warning. Suddenly, the door opened, and a chubby guy with long, wild, straggly hair walked out of the office door. He was about to close the door behind him when a booming voice sounded, "This is the last time! No more chances! We must reach target!"

The chubby guy quickly nodded as he quietly closed the door and turned to face Robert. He surprised Robert when he smiled and gave a quick wink to the new starter as he mimed a playful yawn. Robert looked down at the chubby guy's security pass, which flashed an amber light over his friendly faced photo. Robert quickly read the security pass and offered a smile when he realised this guy worked on the same floor level that he would be working.

Robert was about to start a conversation with his new colleague when he looked up and saw the green light was now flashing above the office door. He smiled and whispered, "That's me, I should go in now."

The chubby guy gave a silent thumbs up to Robert and turned and headed towards the elevators. Robert turned back to the office entrance and slowly pushed open the heavy door and nervously stepped into the room. He could feel the thick carpet beneath his feet as he approached the largest desk he had ever seen in his life. It was made from an expensive dark wood, and on the surface sat several large monitors, all busily arranged like a technological wall on the desk with just a small square gap in the middle.

Robert stood in front of the desk and noticed there was no chair for him to even consider sitting on. The silence of the office was broken by the quick tip-tapping of a keyboard coming from the other side of the monitors. Robert lowered his head to peer through the small square hole that provided a gap between all the glaring screens. A severe square face suddenly appeared within the gap, its head perfectly framed by the square perimeter of the hole as if by specific design. The face carefully stared right at Robert through black thick-rimmed spectacles.

Robert offered a smile to try to break the serious mood, but the silence continued until the square face made a humming sound before saying in a dull flat tone, "Karma. Robert Karma. Age seventeen. Internal logistics. Employment duration, six minutes. Just what have you achieved with DiaboliCo since you joined us?"

Robert was surprised and confused, as he had been expecting a warm welcome from his new company. However, he thought quickly and immediately responded. "Good morning, sir. I have identified an immediate improvement, which will reduce our cost base, increase our customer service, and improve the return to our valued shareholders. The employee manning the front reception desk of this building was breaking company Internet protocol by watching unapproved content on a company computer. In addition, he was making private telephone calls during company hours - delaying visitor management by 90 seconds and potentially damaging the fine reputation of DiaboliCo. We can quickly automate reception services to provide a much more professional twenty-four-hour service, allowing all visitors to schedule appointments with new mobile software that supports self-check-in."

"The investment will pay back in 0.34 months, and we will no longer have to recruit or manage unreliable people in this area. We can even record a personal welcome greeting from you so that all visitors get an personal and warm welcome to DiaboliCo. We should save two million this year, sir, much more if we go global. It's a no-brainer, sir."

Robert wasn't really sure where all those thoughts and words had just come from, but he felt sure it was the type of thing his new leader would want to hear. He stood in silence and awaited a response.

The grim-looking square face offered no reaction and quickly disappeared from the bank of screen monitors. Robert could see a fat finger rapidly prodding numbers into a desktop calculator through the gap in the wall of computer monitors. He heard the continued tapping of the calculator, complemented by a positive-sounding hum. The voice from behind the desk broke the silence.

"Karma, come to my window."

Robert looked around the other side of the desk and could see the outline of a small square figure standing at a large window that filled the end of the office, looking out upon the bustling city. DiaboliCo Tower was the tallest of all the skyscrapers in the city, and it was possible to view the city from far above while feeling close to the clouds. Several helicopters hovered past the window as they prepared to land on various rooftops of the smaller towers below them.

Robert advanced towards the window and noticed that the man he was approaching was smaller than himself in height. As well as having a perfectly square and flat head, his body was broad and box-like and covered in an expensive black business suit. Robert joined the figure at the window, and it was like standing in the cockpit of the world, looking down at everyone in the city, the people and cars below resembling tiny dots that reminded Robert of worker insects.

The CEO stood at the window, looking down at the busy streets below and without turning to Robert he said, "Karma. Welcome to DiaboliCo. You have a simple choice in life. You can either be like those people down in the streets. Stumbling and running from day to day to make ends meet. Or you can get smart and get to where I am. Just look at it all. Just feel this power."

Robert stood and looked down below, impressed by both the view and the encouraging words from Mr Givememore, who then turned to face Robert and asked directly, "So Karma. Are you prepared to give us *absolutely everything*?"

Robert nodded enthusiastically without hesitation as he tried to look into the eyes of Mr Givememore, but only saw his own reflection and the green light from his security pass flash upon the glass surface of the CEO's thick spectacles.

"I'll be watching you personally, Karma. Stay in the green. There is a possible opening on a business critical project if you perform well. Report to level -19 and get to it! I started at the very same level just over 35 years ago, and look where I eventually got to!"

Once again, Robert nodded as he backed away from his senior, who was still standing at the window, admiring his superior view of the city below. As he reversed past the big desk, Robert quickly glanced at the six monitors that glowed out over Mr Givememore's desk. Each screen was displaying moving graphs, flashing numbers, and flowing lists that contained thousands of names that scrolled up the screen at an incredible speed, much too fast for Robert or any other average person to read. Robert also noticed that each name was either displayed in green, amber, or red text. He also saw a thick paper binder that lay next to the computer keyboard. He quickly glanced down and read the title cover of the binder, which read "Company Confidential: Project Karōshi".

He reached the office door and thought against offering any farewell to Mr Givememore. Besides, he could already hear that the CEO was on to his next task and making a phone call. Robert slowly left the office but heard the following words as the thick wooden door slowly eased closed.

"Debbie, it's Number One here. Karma seems a decent prospect. Monitor him closely for fast-track potential. One other small thing for you, terminate all staff who operate the reception desks. In fact, do this in all of our global facilities…Yes, all six thousand of them with immediate effect. Lets call it essential streamlining. Lastly, can you also arrange for my company car to get upgraded, my chauffeur doesn't quite like driving the new Rolls Royce. Make sure the next car includes a wine-chiller. That is all."

Mr Givememore thought about Robert Karma. *Jeez, that kid reminds me of someone.*

Shanghai Times

Established 1802

Best selling newspaper in Asia Pacific

no 201.678

Body discovered, confirmed as Changpu Yamanuchi

Following his mysterious disappearance 5 years ago, the body discovered on a beach off the South China sea has now been confirmed as Changpu Yamanuchi. Local police believe he died at sea, and his body was eventually washed onto the beach of a small remote fishing village.

Mr. Yamanuchi was known as the father of modern robotics and is reported to have been the wealthiest man in the world. It is estimated that there are now over 4 million Yamanuchi robots currently used in factories around the world.

Police have now closed the missing person investigation. The Yamanuchi Research labs were closed 5 years ago, and have since been converted into private luxury 1 person apartments.

Mr. Yamanuchi was a reclusive and private person who dedicated his life to robotic development following a difficult childhood. We understand Mr. Yamanuchi does not have any family and his funeral will be a private ceremony. Guests are not expected.

YAMANUCHI ROBOTICS

Yamanuchi Robotics market reaction :
Share price remains unchanged

New report : Obesity now reaches global crisis | People losing the ability to laugh

19
Meet The Tickleschwings

The elevator stopped, and the blue digital number above its opening door indicated that Robert had reached level -19. He wondered just how far underground he actually was. *There were probably coal mines that didn't go this deep into the earth surface,* he thought.

He stepped out into the stark white corridor, and it felt very different to level 162, from where had just arrived. Down below it felt colder and surprisingly noisy. He could hear people walk around the concrete floors – level -19 did not boast the plush thick carpets of level 162 – and could also hear the throbbing hums coming from the air conditioning units and long fluorescent light strips that hung from the grey concrete ceilings. Robert had watched many movies and thought that level -19 looked like an air raid bunker or underground tomb. He made his way along the corridor that was lined with doors on either side and read the nameplates on each of the tired chalky white office doors. He was impressed and intrigued by some of the job titles that he read below each nameplate. He smiled and giggled as he quietly whispered what he read on one door:

Henry J. Turnipseed III
Global Vice President of Photo Copier Paper (A4 only)

His private laughter was interrupted by a new voice that started from his side, "Isn't that a doozie? I mean, I don't even know what a turnip seed looks like? Do you?"

Robert turned to see the familiar face of the chubby guy he had earlier bumped into on level 162, and once again read the security pass, which said "William Tickleschwing Jnr". The chubby guy glanced down at his own security pass and pouted his bottom lip out as he was reminded that it was still slowly flashing an amber light above his goofy photo. He paused for a moment as he studied his own security pass credentials before looking up at Robert and saying, "I think I must have been on amber for three straight months now. It only needs to flash red ten times, and it's an instant dismissal around here. Ten red flashes and bang! Security is here to escort you right out the building. I once got eight red flashes before I got it back to amber. Close call! Anyways, you can call me Billy Jnr. Welcome to Hell, my friend! Let me show you to your corporate prison cell!"

Robert wasn't sure how to react to such a weird welcome from his new work colleague but politely smiled and followed Billy Jnr down the long corridor. He noticed Billy Jnr walked with a confident and happy strut, almost as if he was walking without a care in the world. They passed several people along the corridor, and Billy Jnr greeted each one by name and enthusiastically wished them a great day. Everyone seemed to smile when they passed Billy Jnr and seemed more than happy to return a greeting. Billy Jnr was dressed very informally but looked perfectly comfortable in his casual attire and his own skin. He wore old running shoes, which Robert suspected had never been used for running or any other form of exercise. An old stretched grey sweatshirt rested on his faded blue jeans, and Robert noticed what seemed like a white dusting that covered Billy Jnr's sweatshirt sleeves. From behind, Billy Jnr could have easily have been mistaken for a plump woman. His wild, frizzy shoulder-length hair that was different from the typical short, smart haircuts of all the other men in the office.

"Here we go, Karma! Your own private hellhole!" Billy Jnr chuckled as he tapped on a shabby white door.

"Oh, Daddeeeeeeee? May we enter? Mr Karma is here for underpants inspection!" Billy Jnr laughed out aloud at his own bad joke as he playfully elbowed Robert in the ribs as the office door opened. It revealed a tall skinny grey man who looked incredibly grave and business-like and who was wearing black thick-rimmed spectacles. He wore an immaculate grey business suit that covered a crisp white cotton shirt and a plain grey tie. Robert guessed this man felt proud of working for DiaboliCo, as pinned to his suit lapel he wore a gold DiaboliCo company badge. The skinny man pitifully shook his head, which hosted a perfectly manicured grey side-parted hairstyle, as Billy Jnr continued to giggle away at the doorway. Then the older man turned to Robert with a serious deadpan expression that would be most useful whenever playing poker.

"Forgive my son. He can't help himself. I am William Tickleschwing Snr. Global Vice President of flip charts at DiaboliCo.

You must be Robert Karma?"

Robert nodded as William Ticklschwing Snr waved his arm inside the office door to usher him into a tiny room, which included three old wooden desks with matching wooden chairs. The office felt very cramped, and Robert noticed there was a wall poster masquerading as a window pinned on one of the dull concrete walls. Although it was obviously just an artificial view from the window, it did feature the most stunning view of a dramatic ocean sunset. On another wall hung four computer monitors, each displaying complex graphs, a map of the world with many flashing dots, and quickly changing numbers which Robert did not understand. On the last remaining wall hung various pictures and images that were arranged in a haphazard, random way. The images included several pictures of delicious-looking cakes and pastries mixed with pictures of rock bands, stunning landscapes, and guitars.

William Ticklschwing Snr noticed that Robert was observing the office decoration and said in a monotone voice, "I use the screens to monitor global flip chart usage within the company. We pioneered the system that allows us to accurately model and predict when each flip chart will need to be replaced. Take a look at what's happening in our facility in Perth, Australia."

Robert looked at the map displayed on the screen and found Australia before scanning the map to find Perth. He found it quickly as it featured a flashing amber icon in that exact location.

William Ticklschwing Snr explained, "Perth is just in the middle of a regional marketing meeting and just about to start brainstorming how they can increase market share. Just watch that icon go red in about seven seconds. That means they will be down to the last five sheets of flip chart. When it goes red, we dispatch a rocket drone to the location that will resupply them with a new flip chart within three minutes. Keep watching and marvel at global telemetrics in action!"

Robert watched carefully as the amber dot on the map soon changed to a red flashing dot. On another screen, he could read the words "Location: Perth – Rocket Dispatched". Within a few minutes, the flashing dot on the map returned to a flashing green icon, and the words on the other screen now read "Location: Perth – Resupply Complete."

Robert nodded with an impressed look on his face as William Ticklschwing Snr sat down at his desk with a proud smile of self-importance. The older man looked very formal and folded his arms as he looked up to Robert and added, "It's quite a brilliant system. It's safe to say that DiaboliCo has never experienced the horror of a flip chart shortage in any of our global facilities in all of my thirty-nine years of service. We have over 6,600 global locations, and I can tell you at any point in time just exactly how many flip charts we have in active use around the globe. Now, that's real cutting-edge technology."

He waited to be asked at least one question by Robert and looked quite annoyed when Billy Jnr, who had just revealed a large delicious-looking cream cake from the top drawer of an old filing cabinet, distracted Robert. He wore an impish looking grin as he placed the beautiful-looking cake on the wooden desk. The chubby youth looked at his father and his new colleague as he raised a polished silver cake slice in his hand and announced, "Made this very morning. It's a cherry peach parfait seated on a cinnamon and walnut sponge. Should go great with a nice cup of Sri Lankan tea. Wanna try some, Robert?"

His father, William Tickleschwing Snr, rolled his eyes to the ceiling and tutted. Robert thought the cake looked delicious and didn't want to offend Billy Jnr, who had obviously spent considerable time and effort in producing such a fine specimen of a treat. A few minutes later, and all three of them were sitting at their desks in the small cramped office eating Billy Jnr's delicious cake. Robert was really enjoying the cake and was quietly munching away while Billy Jnr leant back in his chair and rested both his hands on top of his head. He smiled and said to Robert, "So, my friend, this is how things work around here. My dad, the seriously stressed-looking dude in the corner, has worked on level -19 forever, making sure the company never runs out of flip charts. I am his able deputy who covers for him whenever he is not here. The thing is, he hasn't had a day off in thirty-nine years and has always been in the green. Snap him in half and it will read DiaboliCo! I don't have too much to do, so I like to mix with the people, keep them smiling, and let them sample my new baking creations. I bake something new every day, and they all love my stuff. I am the computer genius who set this whole system up and coded the software, but it's okay if my dad wants to claim credit for it. He has an ego to feed, which I, thankfully, do not. God knows what he would do if I ever left him . . . the system would fall over in days!"

Robert now realised that the white dust he had spotted earlier on Billy Jnr's sweatshirt must have been baking flour. He finished eating and pushed the empty plate in front of him before turning to Billy Jnr. "But don't you get bored, Billy? Coming here every day, just like your dad, and worrying about flip charts?"

Just then, William Tickleschwing Snr quickly interjected, "That's the very problem, Mr Karma! William Jnr doesn't care! I have dedicated my working life to flip chart management at DiaboliCo and feel very proud and privileged to provide such a critical service. Young William here is such a disappointment. He just coasts in and out of here as if it doesn't matter. We could have a flip chart outage in Japan right now, and he wouldn't bat an eyelid. He is happy to waste all his time in the kitchen at home making cakes and pastries all the time.

"Such a bright boy, he could head up the technology department if he wanted! Such a brilliant computer programmer, but such a waster."

Billy Jnr wasn't the type to accept any form of criticism, however, and smiled at his father as he coldly responded, "That's right, Dad. You be a good loyal boy. Thirty-nine years of dedicated service and you'll soon get a promotion to level -18! They may even put you in charge of Post-It notes and envelopes one day!"

An awkward silence fell inside the small office. Robert sat between the skinny father and the carefree chubby youth and tapped his fingers as he looked down at the old wooden desktop. After a few moments, Robert noticed that his own security pass was no longer flashing its green light. It was now flashing amber! He stood up in a panic and felt an immediate pang of stress run through his body. He turned to Billy Jnr, who was still leaning back in his chair with his arms cradling the back of his messy head. He chuckled as he bent forward and whispered, "My, my, we are a stressed little bird, aren't we, Robert? Chill it down, man. Chillax. Just jump up and down ten times, and it'll get you back in the green. Movement sensors are part of the monitoring system. I know how every system in DiaboliCo works. Can't keep too still for more than five minutes my friend. It was designed to stop people taking too long for a toilet break."

Robert followed Billy Jnr's instructions and sure enough, after quickly jumping around, the flashing light on his security pass returned to its regular green flashing light. He felt quick relief and never again wanted to feel worried about his performance status at DiaboliCo. He wanted to get to work straight away and turned to William Tickleschwing Snr. "So, what can I do around here?"

20
Minus One in the Garden

Dennis Baccino lowered himself into the old barber's chair that stood on the edge of the frosty canal-side. The old brown leather was almost icy and felt dry and tight. He could feel another winter fast approaching. Lilly Baccino had just made a fresh warm brew and rested a tray carrying the letterbox-red teapot, teacups, and a plate full of amaretti biscuits in front of her husband. She offered a faint smile and remained standing as she poured the tea and said, "Weather forecast says we are in for a cold snap. Minus one, it said. Hope the ducks will be okay. I'll put some extra feed out."

Dennis splashed some cold milk into his teacup and stirred his drink slowly as he glanced around the garden, surveying its various features, wearing half a smile and half a frown. Since Robert had left, things had changed. Velia Rose had changed. UMA had changed. The garden had changed.

"I do hope Robert will be okay," he said as he decided not to take a biscuit from the plate. He had lost his appetite recently. He paused and then continued. "Everyone needs to find their place in life, and I respect the boy for having the ambition and drive to prove himself, but I just hope he doesn't try too hard. I just . . ." His voice trailed away, and he then chose to remain silent.

Lilly nodded in quiet agreement. She looked across to the aviary in the garden and listened to some warbling birdsong. Her eyes remained fixed on the aviary as she remarked, "We have more than eighteen types of birds in that aviary now, Dennis, did you know that?"

Her husband looked frustrated and replied, "Lilly! What's that got to do with what we are talking about? *Maronna Mia!*" Dennis then fell into an uncontrollable coughing fit, triggered by his dramatic reaction.

Lily smiled sympathetically as she added, calmly, "Not all birds migrate. A few, such as partridges, never move more than a kilometre or so from where they were born. These are called sedentary birds. But they are in the minority. Most birds will migrate, Dennis, and most will eventually return. We just have to trust nature."

A canal barge chugged along the cold, still canal as a flight of swallows flew out from the aviary and up into the bright, fresh morning sky. The Baccinos watched in thoughtful silence as the birds flew away into the distance, shrinking to tiny dots as they began their long and dangerous migration to their next temporary home.

Velia Rose began to play her piano inside the summer house, and its sad melancholic sounds reached the old Italian couple sitting beside the chilly canal-side. Since Robert had left, Velia Rose preferred her own company and had stayed inside the summer house over the last few weeks. Lilly knew her granddaughter well, and she could sense her feeling of loss returning once again. Lilly returned her view up into the wintry morning sky.

Velia Rose continued to play her sad composition with her eyes tightly closed. She didn't need to look at her hands while she played, her memories instinctively channelled the music from her.

They had left her at the beach. It was a sunny day at the seaside. They all went that day. Mum, Dad, Granny and Granddad. It was so hot, the ice-cream that young Velia Rose held in her small hand, dripped down and over her happy sticky fingers. She remembered taking Granddads hand, his trouser bottoms rolled up to his knees, as they strolled down the warm sandy beach to meet the cool sea waves. They paddled and laughed as they jumped waves. Velia Rose remembered talking to her Granddad, telling him all about the dangers of sharks and jellyfish. Velia Rose then remembered looking back, beyond the beach, for her parents. All she could see was Granny, standing alone by the ice cream van. That was it. They were gone.

Velia Rose stopped playing and opened her wet eyes. She could see her Granny sitting at the canal-side, staring up into the sky.

It was a pale blue sky, which now looked incredibly empty.

21
Career Opportunity

Each morning at 4:30 a.m., Robert's alarm would wake him from his short and shallow sleep. The same song would play from his mobile device as he quickly showered and dressed for another busy day at DiaboliCo. Every morning was like a photocopy of the previous day. He would leave his tiny (but very expensive) one-room apartment that was nestled on the sixtieth floor of a residential tower block. He had recently calculated that more than two thousand people must live in this tower block, but for the last few months, he had not met any neighbours or even had a discussion with anyone else.

Every resident seemed comfortably detached as they silently entered the big building, staying alone and perfectly isolated inside their own little box of an apartment. Robert didn't care too much about the lack of community or absence of social interaction, as he was now totally consumed with his new working life.

He had become highly organised. He was a devoted user of a personal planning app. Every day, including voluntary weekend work, he strictly followed the same daily agenda:

04:30 Alarm call. Wake-up. Check for any critical email or messages.
04:31 Shower + teeth.
04:45 Dress (dark suit, white shirt, red tie, black socks)
04:50 Leave apartment/check emails and messages on walk to tube station
04:59 Tube train to work (reply to emails)
05:50 Arrive at train station/grab cheeseburger
06:00 Arrive at work! (revert to my busy work schedule and personal To Do list)
09:01 Billy Jnr (complimentary pastry)
12:00 Lunch at desk (five minutes)
16:01 Billy Jnr (complimentary cake)
20:00 Leave work (if work complete and okay to do so)
20:10 Tube train home/grab cheeseburger supper/check email and messages

21:01	Return to apartment/catch-up on emails and messages
22:00	Iron my work clothes for the following day
22:15	Catch-up on social media
23:00	Wind-down time – play on the games console or watch TV. Teeth.
01:00	Bed. Check email and messages. Set Alarm.
01:30	Sleep

Robert liked the predictable daily routine as it helped him feel in control and avoided any surprises. It was dark when he left his home each morning, and dark when he returned each evening. He had recently worked for two weeks solid without seeing any natural daylight. He had laughed when Billy Jnr compared modern working life to like being a zombie or vampire. *Billy Jnr just didn't get it,* thought Robert. Absolute and total professional dedication to corporate objectives were essential if you wanted to be successful in life.

Robert never stopped to think about whether he was happy with his new life, he was just too busy and work-focused to worry about such things. It seemed to him that most other people in the city lived a very similar existence. Every day, he would catch the train at the same time, sit in the same train carriage, and look at the same people. No one ever talked to each other, as that would be rude or disturb them from their mobile devices.

Most of the train passengers wore personal headphones to help signal to others that they most certainly were not available for any form of social interaction. Headphones acted like an invisible "Person Closed" sign, hanging over someone's face. The headphone users mostly closed their eyes or slept, which completed the temporary detachment from human civilisation.

In his first few weeks, Robert would often wonder why no one ever smiled in the city. But he gradually convinced himself that city professionals were not here to have fun; they were here to get things done, make things happen, and to create shareholder value (whatever that meant). Pretty soon, he felt just like everyone else in the busy city. He no longer smiled. There was just too much other stuff to think or worry about.

Things were going very well at DiaboliCo for Robert. He had continually stayed "in the green" and was given increasingly important senior tasks to perform. At first, he was kept busy delivering mail and small packages to all the various departments within DiaboliCo Tower. Operating within the massive building, he got to see how the business worked and was always suggesting ideas to help improve things. Every Friday evening at 7 p.m., all employees who had stayed "in the green" for a full week would receive a small bonus payment. The bonus payments got bigger if you stayed "in the green" for months, or even years. Most people worked longer and harder to stay "in the green", as the required performance target always increased in line with corporate objectives.

The Tickleschwings liked Robert and enjoyed sharing the small office on level -19. William Snr admired Robert's dedication and strong work ethic. He reminded William Snr of his younger self in that he was self-motivated and hungry to prove himself, always willing to give everything to the company.

William Snr didn't often dwell on his own career progress at DiaboliCo. He had been a loyal and devoted servant to the company for more than thirty-nine years, but he still worked on level -19. At least he hoped to enjoy a modest retirement when he reached his seventieth birthday. He couldn't help compare Robert with his son, Billy Jnr. His son was so intelligent and comfortable with people but was destined for a lifelong career on level -19 as he refused to play by the company rules. It hurt William Snr when he heard someone at the office call his son "the perfect slacker". They were right.

Billy Jnr really appreciated Robert's help too, as it allowed him to do even less. As a reward for Robert, each day Billy Jnr would bake delicious treats for Robert to taste-test. Billy Jnr was not a serious person, but Robert noticed how Billy Jnr would eagerly await his reaction to a new cake, biscuit, or pastry recipe. He would even make secret private notes of Robert's tasting comments, but Robert had noticed he made sure no one thought he cared too much about his baking skills. Billy Jnr wanted everyone to believe he was just a cool dude who didn't care too much about anything. But Robert knew he loved baking.

Robert had been working hard at the company for exactly three months when he received the order to report immediately to Mr Givememore on level 162. He entered the elevator and felt worried that something must be wrong as he moved silently upwards within the massive concrete tower. The elevator doors opened at level 162 and just as before, a group of serious business suits, all wearing thick-rimmed glasses, entered the lift as Robert made his way along the thick-carpeted corridor.

The door to Mr Givememore's office was already wide open and above the doorway was a slowly flashing green light. Robert was about to gently tap on the open door when Mr Givememore quickly appeared right in front of him. The small square man wore a broad beaming smile as he took Robert's hand and shook it with a vigorous intensity. The small boxy executive still managed to maintain his full smirk as he welcomed Robert to his office.

"Well done, Karma! Good job! I just knew it! Let's take a look at your personal analytics on the media wall just at the end, by my window. Great numbers, Karma – let me show you!"

Robert felt a mix of relief that Mr Givememore seemed happy but also felt a suspicious confusion as he was ushered through the luxury wood-panelled office. They reached a large blank white wall and stood before it as Mr Givememore quietly cleared his throat before making his verbal instruction to the media wall.

"Show employee analytics. Employee location - DiaboliCo Tower."

The blank wall quickly came to life and displayed an impressive range of colourful complex graphs and infographics. Robert did not understand what any of this meant, and his confusion grew as Mr Givememore grew in giddy excitement as he requested a new screen view.

"Show employee detail. Employee name – Karma, Robert."

The screen refreshed with another view of complex numbers and graphs.

"Wow! Just wow, Karma! You are almost off the chart, my boy! Our data tells me that you are the highest performing employee in the last three months! You have worked longer hours than anyone else, stayed green since day one, highly punctual, take the fewest toilet breaks and best still, you earn the lowest salary in the whole building! What's more, you have made many positive improvements to the business. Your average email response time is quite impressive at twenty-eight seconds. On average, you answer your phone after 1.8 seconds. I'm sure we can improve on that, but still, it's all very encouraging!"

Mr Givememore put his hand around Robert's shoulder and firmly patted him like an obedient dog. He continued, "You sent 131,061 emails in your first three months, Karma. What an excellent metric! You should feel very proud. To reward your fantastic contribution, we will put your name in the monthly global newsletter. Quite an honour, my boy."

Robert stood still as he watched his animated boss bounce over to his desk to collect the binder that he recognised from his last visit to the office. It was the binder titled: "Company Confidential: Project Karōshi".

Within a millisecond, the expression on Mr Givememore's face switched from being deliriously happy to a look of grave seriousness. He moved slowly closer to Robert, his thick-rimmed spectacles disguising his penetrating cutting stare. Robert felt the whole mood swing in just a few moments as Mr Givememore tapped his small fat finger on the binder in his hands. He continued slowly prodding the binder with increasing force as he whispered, "This, Karma, is *the* next big thing at DiaboliCo. Project Karōshi will transform this company and generate at least 1.17% additional gross profit to our shareholders. I am asking you to lead this secret project, Karma. I know you can do it, but do *you* know you can do it?"

Without even asking for more details, Robert was already nodding his acceptance of his new task. Mr Givememore slowly produced a satisfied smile, which revealed his very many perfectly square-shaped teeth. The senior executive moved uncomfortably close to Robert's face, as he muttered, "Make a success of this, and you could be fast-tracked to Vice President before you know it. How does that sound, Karma? Bigger salary, private health plan, company car, personal pension, loyalty bonus if you stay for thirty years, four days' annual leave, dental cover, business suit allowance, the whole shebang! Do you want to live and taste the dream, Karma? How bad do you want it, boy?"

Robert was still nodding as he replied, calmly, "I want it all, Mr Givememore, and I will give DiaboliCo everything to get it."

Mr Givememore studied Robert in silence for a few moments, smirking and slowly nodding before turning his attention back to the media wall. *Jeez, this kid reminded him of his younger self.* He then barked another command at the wall. "Show me planned employee terminations." A long list of over 100 employee names, all in a blood-red text, displayed on the media wall. Robert quickly scanned the list as Mr Givememore slowly tutted, shaking his boxlike head as he walked closer to the screen.

"I'll deal with these losers while you get Project Karōshi up and running. You will find the project brief in the binder. You can take a spare office up here on level 162, as you will need to work closely with me. My personal assistant, Chantelle Golddigger, can help you with anything you need. I am expecting big things from you, Karma!

Do not fail me."

Robert was still listening to Mr Givememore but was quite distracted by the red names he read on the termination list. Halfway down the list, his eyes locked on one name.

William Tickleschwing Jnr.

22
Project Karoshi

Robert returned to level -19 and entered the small office as William Tickleschwing Snr monitored flip chart usage trends in the Asia Pacific region. Billy Jnr was stood in the corner, excitedly slicing an awesome and very thick red velvet cake that he had made at home.

Robert sat at his desk and quickly hid the confidential project binder in his desk drawer. While he was in the cluttered top drawer, he grabbed and retrieved an old tatty dictionary. He thumbed through the soft pages and eventually found the word he was seeking:

Karōshi
(過労死)
noun
1.
(in Japan) death caused by overwork

Robert could feel his heart sink as he read the dictionary definition. What on earth was this project all about? Whatever it was, he didn't feel good about it. His mood didn't improve much, even when Billy Jnr placed an enormous slice of red velvet cake on Robert's desk. Robert looked up at a proud-looking Billy Jnr standing at his desk and offered him a false smile that Billy read through immediately. Billy Jnr motioned Robert to eat the cake in front of him.

"The buttercream is the secret with this one, pal. People think it's the red sponge, but that's just for show, it's all about the delicious gooey buttercream taste. Try it. It will help you relax and tell me what's on your crazy little ambitious mind, my friend."

Robert could not help but giggle as Billy Jnr followed this up by pulling a crazy, goofy expression as he passed another slice of cake to his disapproving father, who was still quietly and totally engrossed by flip chart consumption patterns in Taiwan.

Robert tasted the cake, and it was indeed most delicious. The buttercream tasted incredible. He thought about complimenting Billy Jnr, who now sat with both arms tightly folded, eagerly awaiting his tasting comments. He noticed that Billy Jnr's security pass was still flashing its usual amber light.

"Just how long have you been flashing amber, Billy?" asked Robert.

"What about the cake, man? Forget about work performance for just one second! Did you like the buttercream filling?" replied a frustrated Billy Jnr.

"The cake was great, Billy. You know, they could terminate you on the spot if you hit red. You are *so* close to real trouble. It's not as if you aren't smart. What's so wrong about toeing the company line?"

Billy Jnr dropped his head and shook it slowly. He sat in silence for a few moments before slowly raising a finger and pointing straight across the small office at his father, William Tickleschwing Snr. The older man was now frantically tapping at his keyboard to help avoid a flip chart outage in the Philippines. Robert looked across at Billy Jnr, who now wore no expression at all. Robert had never seen Billy look so honest, real, and severe.

"Because I'm terrified of turning into him." Billy Jnr said, his sorry eyes and pointed finger still locked on his distressed father.

That evening, Robert waited for both of the Tickleschwings to leave the office before he retrieved the Project Karōshi binder from his desk drawer. It was now 19:45 p.m. and Robert sat alone at his desk on level -19 as he opened the binder, expecting to find a long and detailed instruction of what the project entailed. Instead, he was surprised to find just one torn page of company letter-headed notepaper sitting on the top of a thick wedge of papers. The torn page contained just a few typed words and numbers. Although it took Robert just a few seconds to read it, he re-read it again and again as he sat alone in the office, buried nineteen levels below the ground.

He understood the project requirement, but he had no idea of how to achieve it. He felt quite alone with the problem and could already feel an unhealthy pressure building up inside. Elsewhere in the binder was a comprehensive list of all employee names along with their age, performance rating, and current salary. Robert kept returning to the word "headcount". He knew it was a business term that really meant "people". Of course, no one liked saying that the company needed to cut people, as that just sounded mean and inhumane. It was much easier to use an alternative business term like headcount reduction. Different words, but the same outcome.

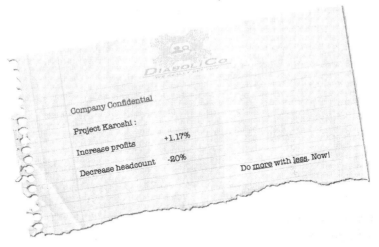

Robert took a last look around the small office on level -19 before he packed his personal effects in to a small brown cardboard box. He looked up at the bright screen monitors on the wall, noticing that the company had adequate global supplies of flip charts to cover another thirty-eight hours. He smiled and shrugged to himself, switching the light off and leaving the cramped office on level -19. His time had now arrived to move on up in the world, and that's just what he did as he pressed the elevator button for level 162. In just one minute, Robert Karma had already moved 1.2 miles up in the world.

He stepped out on to level 162 and confidently nodded as he passed a fat bearded man wearing thick-rimmed spectacles. The thick, lush carpet felt good beneath Roberts's self-assured steps. Robert found his new office and firmly closed the door behind him. The sign on his office door read:

Mr Robert Karma
Global Project Lead: Project Karōshi

23
Tranſitionſ & Acquiſitionſ

It didn't take long for Robert to feel at home on level 162. Every day, he would stand at his large office window that faced out on to the busy city, enjoying the sunshine that radiated through the hovering city smog. In just a few days, he had completely forgotten about the people working below ground level at DiaboliCo who did not enjoy any natural sunlight. He was just too busy to think about anyone else.

Mr Givememore was especially delighted with Robert's progress. In just a few weeks, he had made a very encouraging start to Project Karōshi. He had quickly introduced various ways to reduce costs and headcount at the company. This included the introduction of a new performance policy, which incorporated the instant termination of any employee who took more than three minutes to respond to an email or text. Some people just couldn't handle the stress, and some others were just too slow. Those changes led to hundreds of people leaving the company in just a few weeks. It didn't matter to Mr Givememore. All he cared about was increased productivity of the people who remained, employee number reduction, and increasing the profit margin for the company.

Robert would meet Mr Givememore every morning at 6 a.m., and they excitedly discussed new profit improvement ideas. Mr Givememore could see real management potential with Robert and had offered to personally mentor him to ensure he imparted help and advice to *his* promising young business executive.

Robert could feel a rapid change in himself. His confidence and ego soared as he received numerous compliments, as well as bigger performance bonus payments from Mr Givememore. He started to feel powerful as he looked down on the city from his office at the top of the tower. Robert recognised that he needed to *look* successful as well, so he invested in some expensive tailored business suits, silk ties, and the best shirts and shoes. He had also decided to style his hair so that he looked more serious and professional. It had an impact, as he had noticed an increased level of attention coming from the gorgeous Chantelle Golddigger, who sat in the office next to Robert.

"Good morning, Mr Karma. Lovely hair. Great threads. Love the shoes. No wonder you are Number One's favourite," said the smiling Chantelle as Robert arrived at the office.

Robert didn't know quite how to respond and chose to return just a shy and humble smile. This only seemed to encourage the curvy blonde secretary to continue.

"I mean, talk about hot property. Your own executive level office and being personally mentored by Number One himself. You are certainly going places, Mr Karma. You are so, so awesome!"

Like a cunning predator, Chantelle Golddigger rose from behind her desk and confidently strolled over to Robert as he stood in the doorway of his office, his back turned while he fumbled for his key to open the office door. Chantelle casually tapped him on the shoulder, and even before he turned around, Robert was almost overwhelmed by the musky thick floral scent of her expensive French perfume.

He turned to look at Chantelle, who was now standing uncomfortably close. She was at least ten years older than Robert but seemed very interested in her younger colleague. She was very pretty and looked like a celebrity model Robert had seen on a recent TV show – *Save Me, I'm a Shameless Celebrity*. Chantelle raised her hands to slowly adjust Robert's red silk tie. She smirked mischievously as Robert stood rooted to the spot and then gave him a final nod of approval.

"I can see great things happening for you, Mr Karma. A girl like me could be one of those great things. Think about it, but not for too long. Number One wants to see you right now," Chantelle whispered as she moved closer to Robert, close enough for her to breathe warmly on his face before she turned and prowled back to her desk.

Within a few moments, Robert was in the office of Mr Givememore and felt a little relieved to escape the very direct attention of Chantelle. He did think she was pretty, though, and wondered if they could look good together. He imagined her with him in an open-top sports car, or in an exclusive restaurant, or at a fashionable and exclusive nightclub where the rich and famous partied. He quickly concluded that she could make him look even more successful to other people.

Mr Givememore, who was sitting in his large leather chair, suddenly interrupted Robert's imagination by shouting, "Karma! I had the most brilliant idea last night. Let's call it an employee benefit for now. It came to me like a gift from the profit gods. The shareholders will love it. Even the stupid employees will think they like it! I will need your help in getting it up and running, but trust me, it's the future!" The small square CEO was visibly excited and could hardly contain himself.

"But first, Karma, let's take a look at Project Karōshi. You said you had a new idea that can help us do more with less. Talk to me." Mr Givememore barked as his face changed from jovial colleague to sinister boss within three seconds.

"Well, sir," Robert replied, "I had a look at the performance monitoring system and noticed that some employees could operate at amber level for weeks or even months. They still feel safe because they are not in the red. We need to increase the employee fear. Too many people are coasting at amber level."

Mr Givememore nodded attentively, grinning as he basked in the thought of creating more fear among his employees. He waited for Robert to continue.

"So with just a minor adjustment, sir, we could bypass the amber status. Employees who are not operating at green will go straight to red termination status. They will have just one minute to rectify the performance issue. If they fail to comply, they are terminated with immediate effect. I conducted an analysis last night, sir, and we could expect to lose around 700 sub-standard employees within the next month. No redundancy payment is necessary as the termination is due to poor performance.

"It's perfectly legal, sir. I had the lawyers review it all. I think we can save about 42 million a year going forward, sir. Profit levels will increase by 0.0034%."

Mr Givememore leapt from his large leather chair like he was celebrating a lottery win. He performed an awkward little dance but didn't seem to care. He bounced across to Robert and shook his hand. "Genius, Karma! You have a quite brilliant business mind! Jeez, you remind me so much of my younger self! Let's implement it today so that profits can increase as soon as possible. Don't bother with employee communications. Let them experience a few live terminations up close and personal! That will increase the fear and stress levels and make them work harder. Another rather serious cash bonus is coming your way, Karma! We always reward excellence at DiaboliCo!"

Robert left his very animated boss and returned to his own office to start making the changes they had just discussed and agreed. If he stopped to think about it, he knew many people would lose their jobs at DiaboliCo. But as he started tapping away on his keyboard and entering system access codes, he told himself, "It's just business. Winners and losers. Sorry, but that's just the way it works."

Within five minutes, he had reconfigured the performance monitoring system and had scheduled it to remove the amber status at 2 p.m. Robert wondered if he would hear the squeals from the many employees who would be collectively terminated from the company at that particular time. He didn't think about this for too long, though, as his mind was distracted by the website he was browsing on his computer screen.

He was looking at three different glossy sports cars that filled the screen – two of them were in a warm red colour, and the other one was in a cold metallic blue. He impulsively clicked buy on the icon flashing below the blue sports car. His latest bonus payment could cover the deposit required, and he felt sure he wouldn't have any problem covering the monthly payments for the next 380 months. Anyhow, the cost didn't matter much to Robert. It was all about projecting the right professional image. He needed to show others just what a great success he was, and an expensive sports car was the most visible badge of success he could think of. The car would get delivered in the next few days, and that should give him enough time to arrange a date with his next planned badge of success: Chantelle.

Of course, a sports car would also need a garage to keep it safe and secure in a city full of watchful criminal eyes. Robert flicked through various city property websites to find a new penthouse apartment in the city. It needed to be upmarket, in the popular area of the city. He quickly found the apartment he wanted. It was close to the office and all the fashionable bars and clubs. It featured spectacular views of the city, and it had a wall-size television, wet room, Internet-connected kitchen and many other state-of-the-art features. The rent was incredibly expensive, but Robert didn't worry about that. He needed a place that was appropriate for a successful and ruthless business executive. He started to complete the online application form for the new apartment and was already thinking of various stuff to fill it with. He hadn't even noticed when the time passed 2 p.m.

He completed his online application and then smiled shrewdly at his PC monitor screen when it flashed a large "CREDIT APPROVED! YOU CAN NOW MOVE-IN!" notification message.

Among the flashing numbers and metrics displayed on the screen, he noticed the outline of his own reflection within the screen's glare. For a moment, he thought the outline shape of his head looked square, like a box, before his flitting puddle-deep attention moved back to reviewing the profit analysis metrics.

***

Mr A.U. Givememore sat alone at his desk and smiled at his computer screens, nodding with silent approval as he secretly monitored the activity of Robert Karma. *Jeez, that boy reminded him of his younger self.* He was already developing nice expensive tastes, the apartment he had just applied for was in a very affluent part of the city. Pretty soon the boy might realise that he would have to work longer and harder if he wanted more of the good stuff.

The senior executive stood and moved over to his office window, lighting a thick cigar as he looked down at the bustling city. He recalled how he had joined DiaboliCo when he was Robert Karmas age. Mr Givememore recalled his own extreme hunger for success which was driven by a desire to prove himself. His parents never expected much from him. His father was a career military man who never seemed impressed by his hard working son. Mr Givememore never won a crumb of approval from his father. His mother didn't have much interest in her only son either and seemed to spend most of her time at work. She was a very dull woman who quite enjoyed inspecting thousands of toilet seats that were made at a local factory. Mr Givememore only ever remembered seeing her smile when she talked about toilet seat quality control measures.

Mr Givememore realised long ago what had driven him to be a big city hot shot. He had worked his way to the very top of the tree to try and win the love and attention of his parents. He had made *every sacrifice* to get to the top and to show them that he could be a success. A son to celebrate and to feel proud about. Mr Givememore just wanted to show his parents that he was worthy of their love and attention.

It never came. Never even close. And so he chose wealth and power to fill that empty void in his life.

Mr Givememore sucked heavily on his thick cigar. The dark toxic nicotine smoke filled his sour and angry insides, but he didn't worry about that. He knew he was already full of poison that came from somewhere else.

24
The Broken Teapot

Dennis Baccino sat alone in the old barber's chair perched at the water's edge. He had smiled and waved at the few barges that gently passed by and had enjoyed the time of quiet reflection. Lilly and Velia Rose were both inside the house preparing dinner, and UMA had left the garden earlier that morning to help out at a local refuge centre for homeless people. For the last few months, the little robot had been taking unsold or nearly out-of-date food from the local supermarket and taking it to the shelter. If UMA didn't do this, then all the food would be sent for disposal at a local landfill site. Dennis shook his head as he thought about how the big companies could just throw billions of tonnes of food away every week, while millions of people went without food. *Such a crazy world, not enough empathy,* the old man thought to himself.

He leant forward from the barber's chair and reached for the gramophone. The turn handle of the old Symphola gramophone was cold to the touch as he operated the old but reliable wind-up contraption. The old oak casing of the old sound box was still intact, but its warm oak colour had now faded, and its dried-out edges had started to warp and twist. Dennis rested the gramophone arm on the thick black vinyl record and there was a crackle before classical music began to flow from its brass horn. He learned back in the old barber's chair and rested his tired head, pulling a soft tartan blanket that Lilly had brought him over himself as the sweeping violin strings filled his mind. One of his favourite songs washed through his thoughts as he gave a gentle deep sigh and softly sang in a voice that was both faltering and fading away.

"E aspetto l'orizzonte per sempre, solo per essere con te ancora una volta..." (And I will wait on the horizon forever, just to be with you once again...)

A few minutes later, the old man was now very still and silent. No longer did his exhaled breath create a puff of steam in the chilled morning air. The gramophone needle had reached the end of the recording and now just sounded a lonely empty crackle. A canal barge chugged past the lifeless figure reclined in the chair at the side of the canal. It was the only time that Dennis Baccino had not waved and shared a friendly smile with a passing stranger.

The red teapot fell from the tray and smashed as it hit the wooden decking. Lilly Baccino had reached her husband but immediately knew he was not taking his usual nap in the old barber chair. His face seemed relaxed, almost smiling, and fully at peace. She dropped everything, almost fainting, as she reached out to hold on to him. Velia Rose had heard the teapot crash to the ground and raced out from her summer house. She joined her grandmother, who was now silently sobbing into the cold tartan blanket that covered Dennis. They both cradled the old man, recognising that he was gone and beyond rescue.

Lilly stroked his silver hair and said quietly, "Dennis . . . *prego non lasciarmi sola.*" (Please do not leave me alone.)

The old barber's chair turned and revolved on its stand as both of them held him tight. The heavyset silver footrest of the barber chair silently swivelled and knocked the garden table, jolting it so much that the table tilted and lost all of its contents. Mrs Baccino and Velia Rose turned and watched in a fresh wave of agony as the old Symphola gramophone slowly slid off the table and down into the cold, murky waters of the canal. Lilly Baccino stood upright, now lost in complete shock as she looked down into the canal. She watched as the old brass horn gradually disappeared from view, watching her wedding present sink below the water's surface. The horn's familiar glistening bright gold now drifted into a cloudy darkness.

25
Employee Benefits

Robert and a group of bespectacled executives joined an animated Mr Givememore in the elevator. They all stood smiling and cozied around the short and loud CEO as he barked out his instruction. "Take me to level -20! It's grand opening day! Do it now! Let's do this thing!"

The elevator took them down to the lowest part of DiaboliCo Tower. The elevator doors opened at level -20 to a large expectant crowd of DiaboliCo employees, all of them standing in front of a long red ribbon that hung before a temporary screen that displayed the company logo and its tagline – "We really get you!".

Mr Givememore smiled as he exited the elevator and while scanning the waiting crowd, quickly raised his small square hands to start applauding himself. This then triggered his waiting audience to join the applause, which included a few enthusiastic whoops from his highly compliant spectators. He then produced an incredible piece of acting as he perfected an expression of humble surprise when he reached the speaker's podium that stood by the hanging red ribbon. He smiled and nodded as the applause continued to inflate his ego before he slowly raised his hands to quieten the onlookers. He stepped up on to a small crate that stood behind the podium, allowing him to reach the microphone and appear of normal height. Mr Givememore still managed to maintain his broad grin as he addressed the crowd of employees stood before him.

"Wow! You guys! Just wow! This is what makes DiaboliCo the best company in the world!"

The crowd cheered and once again provided an enthusiastic applause. Mr Givememore was highly experienced in public speaking and allowed a long silence to fill the room as everyone waited for him to continue. His expression changed as he looked around the room and silently nodded at familiar employees. He now looked quite emotional and solemn as he clenched his right fist and slowly pounded his chest as he resumed his speech.

"You guys! That's what DiaboliCo is all about – you guys!

Making it happen every day – you guys! Taking the company to new heights – you guys! You guys are everything!"

The crowd erupted into wild applause again as Mr Givememore randomly pointed to various employees in the crowd while mouthing a silent thank-you.

"Like all great relationships, the love has got to flow from both parties, and we are here today to share an exciting new employee benefit with you all. It's critical that we take care of our company's greatest asset: you!"

Once again, the crowd whooped its delight.

"We recognise that modern life is tough and demanding. We know how much you all sacrifice to help the company succeed. We appreciate you can sometimes feel locked to your desk or at your workstation, never getting away to do the things you really want to do. I really feel your pain and frustration. Well, now it's time to correct that and give you all something back as a token of our appreciation! More than anything, we care about your personal health and wellbeing. Without you guys, we don't have a great company."

Mr Givememore then grabbed an oversized pair of scissors that lay on the podium and suddenly bounced down from the crate he was standing on. He stood before the temporary screen as he raised the wide scissor blades up to the hanging red ribbon.

"Dear colleagues, I give you the latest DiaboliCo innovation in employee benefits!"

Robert joined in the applause and then realised he was now standing next to both of the Tickleschwings. He had not spoken to either of them for a few months, and he felt genuinely happy to see them. The Tickleschwings did not return his smile, however, but instead politely nodded. Robert was relieved to see that Billy Tickleschwing Jnr's security pass was now flashing at green, but he also noticed that Billy Jnr now looked quite formal and almost grey. He was wearing a shirt and tie and sporting a smart haircut, and he now looked much like the other employees.

The crowd erupted again as Mr Givememore snipped the ribbon while the screen behind him fell away to reveal an amazing sight. Emphatic energetic rock music played out loudly from hidden speakers as the crowd of employees went wild while some indoor fireworks exploded confetti-like glitter into the air. Most of the crowd cheered before they even took a close look at the strange new equipment that filled level -20.

It was an employee gym with a difference. As far as the eyes could see on level -20, there were seemingly endless rows of large grey metal treadwheels. Hundreds of round metal cages, perfectly aligned in straight rows, the gaps between them providing perfectly straight corridors. Robert moved closer to inspect a treadwheel, and as he did so, Mr Givememore made another announcement – one that Robert did *not* expect.

"Ladies and gentlemen, I would like to introduce Mr Robert Karma. A highly gifted young man and very much the future of DiaboliCo. He is here to demonstrate our innovation, the E-Z Station 3000!"

The crowd yelped and cheered as Robert flashed a surprised look to Mr Givememore, who returned a sly smile while motioning him to enter the E-Z Station 3000. Robert complied with his leader as he turned and stepped on to the cool metal wheel that was in a locked position. He stood within the wheel as Mr Givememore provided a running commentary of the E-Z Station 3000.

"The E-Z Station is a new innovation brought to you by DiaboliCo. It allows you, employees, to do it all. Multi-tasking has never been easier while employees get critical exercise. No need to lose time after work by going to the gym! Work out while you work with the E-Z Station 3000!"

The crowd gave another standing ovation as Mr Givememore grinned and motioned Robert to turn sideways so that he was now facing the inside of the metal wheel.

"The E-Z Station 3000 is fully voice-activated and recognises over 140 languages. Please, Mr Karma, ask it nicely to activate."

Robert stood on the still metal wheel and said, calmly, "Activate now."

The E-Z Station 3000 came to life, and several things happened very quickly. A white light shone down from above the wheel as a large hydraulic metal arm rose up from the side of the wheel. The metal arm stopped in a vertical position that reached Robert's waist. The arm then mechanically unfolded a mini desk in front of where he stood. On the desk was a laptop that automatically opened itself to reveal its keyboard. The E-Z Station 3000 whirred as a mechanical rod lowered a telephone headset on to Robert's head. Another metal arm with a camera fitted to its end automatically dropped into a position that was just a few feet from his face. The camera had three flashing lights above the camera lens: green, amber, and red.

Robert suddenly heard a loud click and realised that the

treadwheel was now unlocked and able to turn freely. He slowly walked within the metal wheel as it created a low hum and looked over at Mr Givememore, who was eager to continue his commentary.

"See how the E-Z Station 3000 fits around you? It has more than 3,000 detectors to ensure that you find your optimum most comfortable position before you get to work. It will only start turning, allowing you that priceless exercise, once your devices are all in place. Mr Karma, please commence a gentle jog while using your laptop to email."

Robert quickened his step, and the metal wheel happily accelerated its revolution speed. He lightly jogged on the wheel as he tapped away on his company laptop before sending an email. He turned to the watching crowd and gave them a smile and a thumbs-up gesture. The crowd cheered as Mr Givememore resumed commentary.

"Need to make a phone call? Just use the voice-activated headset to call any global contact. What about video conferencing? You got it!" The laptop in front of Robert went into videoconference mode, and the familiar face of Debbie DeCeiver waved to Robert from the laptop display screen. The crowd once again yelped in joy as Robert talked to Debbie.

"I know what you are all thinking – 'but I have still to leave my desk to eat and drink!' Well, we thought of that too!" Mr Givememore grinned proudly as two transparent tubes were automatically lowered to within touching distance of Robert's face. Giant drinking straws then slowly propelled from both tubes, close enough for him to use while he was still running and working.

"No more need for interfering lunch or coffee breaks! The food and drink tubes operate by voice command. Show them, Karma."

Robert continued to jog as he quickly thought about what refreshments to order. He then told the watching camera, "Food order, liquidised cheeseburger and fries. Drink order, extra strong coffee with cream, no sugar."

Within moments, the order was delivered via the food and drink tube, and it was easy for Robert to consume his order while he ran and worked on the treadwheel. Once again, the watching crowd broke into tumultuous applause as they fist pumped the air in celebration. Robert thought the food tasted disgusting but disguised this opinion by wearing a false smile as he patted his stomach and licked his lips.

Mr Givememore continued from the podium, "Of course, we never forget what made us great, and we know what works really well at DiaboliCo. We ensured that the key features of our brilliant performance monitoring system were fully incorporated within the E-Z Station 3000. Let us demonstrate."

Robert looked up at the camera that was carefully observing his actions. He could feel the camera scanning and monitoring his every move. It slowly flashed its green light while he ran on the treadwheel as he developed a new presentation on the laptop. He could feel the wheel moving increasingly faster as he heard Mr Givememore bellow another instruction to the crowd.

"Now for this part of the demonstration, we will need a willing and loyal DiaboliCo employee. Do we have a willing volunteer?" Mr Givememore scanned the large crowd of enthusiastic employees, many of who were already waving their hand in the air as willing volunteers. He grinned menacingly as he continued to survey the crowd but then quickly changed his expression as he locked his eyes on young Billy Tickleschwing Jnr. Mr Givememore recognised him from previous corrective interviews he had provided. He smirked as he pointed directly at Billy Jnr and announced, "Ah, yes, you, Shicklewing, is it? Yes, you would be just perfect! Please come up here and step into the empty E-Z Station 3000 unit next to Mr Karma."

At this point, William Tickleschwing Senior stepped out in front of his son and moved from the crowd and towards Mr Givememore. He halted as Mr Givememore interjected and blared out from the microphone, "Not you! The demonstration won't work with you. Get back in line. I want him. Yes, you, the fat guy hiding behind his father! Up here now, boy." Mr Givememore jabbed his finger directly at Billy Jnr.

Billy Jnr nervously approached the E-Z Station 3000 and stared meekly at Robert, who was still running within his turning metal wheel. Billy Jnr edged on to the empty wheel next to Robert, looking dejected as he frowned and turned his gaze on the eagerly watching audience. Billy Jnr wore a look of quiet resignation as he raised his head and said, "Activate now."

Just as before, the E-Z Station 3000 that contained Billy Jnr burst into activity as its various mechanisms positioned themselves around its anxious occupant. The camera studied Billy Jnr's face as its green light slowly flashed. Without any further instructions, the wheel started to turn slowly as the laptop began to bleep with several new email notifications. At the same time, Billy Jnr was asked to accept an incoming phone call. The wheel started to accelerate quickly, and another notification appeared on his laptop, this time asking him to accept an invitation to a videoconference.

The food and drink tubes were lowered and rested by Billy Jnr's head, while the laptop was now beeping repeatedly to alert him to order his refreshments. The crowd grew in agitation as some of the employees started to shout to Billy Jnr, who was now looking very lost inside the spinning wheel as the camera light switched to an amber flashing light.

"Speed up dude, you're going too slow! You need to start running faster!"

"Answer that phone call! Don't let it go to answerphone."

"Join the videoconference, man! Hurry up and join or you will miss it!"

"You're going too slow! Order your food and drinks. Hurry it up!"

"You're never going to make target! Go faster for your bonus!"

Billy Jnr looked at the wheel next to him, which contained Robert, now panting as he was almost sprinting within his wheel. Billy Jnr then looked around and found his father's face in the crowd, looking distressed and calling out to him, pleading him to get to work on the EZ Station 3000. Lastly, he looked at Mr Givememore. Billy Jnr fixed his stare on the callous executive and slowly shook his head in pity. Mr Givememore just smiled and nodded gleefully.

Billy Jnr refused to keep up with the treadwheel as it turned faster and ignored the flashing digital alert that now flashed "ACCELERATE NOW". He reached to his laptop and declined both the incoming phone call and the videoconference requests. Then he looked directly into the camera that was monitoring his every move. He smiled as the flashing amber light quickly turned to a flashing red light. It slowly blinked its red light five times before the E-Z Station 3000 suddenly stopped. The wheel stopped spinning, and all of the devices that surrounded Billy Jnr were quickly withdrawn. Billy Jnr stood still as the unit made a deep disapproving beep followed by a computerised voice which made an announcement, "Termination. Non-compliant employee. Error code 962. New recruitment request sent to human resources."

The metal grid where Billy Jnr stood suddenly opened up, and he instantly disappeared from view, falling into the dark hole without a sound. The grid closed itself within a few seconds, and the

E-Z Station 3000 stood empty, waiting silently for its next user. The crowd also went quiet, and William Tickleschwing Snr stood still with his head in his hands. The silent crowd returned its attention to Mr Givememore, who was still at the podium, to conclude his commentary.

"So, we all see what happens if we fail to meet the performance standards required at DiaboliCo? Please always remember that people are our greatest asset. Now, let's return to see how the very able Mr Karma is performing. The system is telling me that Mr Karma has had a very productive session! Fifty-eight emails, fourteen phone calls, and three videoconferences. Excellent! He also ran six miles, so managed to burn 32,000 calories! Well done, Mr Karma, that's another cash bonus for you!" The crowd cheered again when they heard the word bonus.

"That's right, everyone, you all get the chance to earn a monthly cash bonus! This employee benefit is now available to everyone and your payment to enjoy this service will be automatically deducted from your monthly pay. We have worked so hard to make this perfect for you!"

The crowd resumed its raucous cheering as they all madly rushed to try out their very own treadwheel. Within minutes, at least 750 treadwheels were all whirring into action as each employee made phone calls while tapping away on the laptops. Robert stepped away from his treadwheel, almost out of breath from the intensive workout he had just undertaken. He approached Mr Givememore, who was proudly surveying the employees running faster and faster and trying to do more stuff at the same time. The CEO gazed down from his podium and looked fondly at Robert.

"This could be my finest hour, Karma. Just look at them. They really think it's an employee benefit! They are actually paying us while they run on wheels like rats trapped in a cage," he sniggered.

Robert caught an unpleasant whiff of Mr Givememore's foul-smelling breath. "We could improve it, sir," he replied.

Mr Givememore raised an eyebrow and let Robert continue.

"Think about it, sir. With 750 active treadwheels, we are generating 100,000 kilowatts of electricity every hour. That's over 2.4 million kilowatts of electricity a day. That's enough to power this whole building. We wouldn't have to pay an electricity company to power DiaboliCo Tower. We can do it ourselves! We will save at least twenty million a year and get healthier employees. It's also a clean energy source, so DiaboliCo can win exclusive industry awards for being caring environmentalists. I can find a way to connect the treadmill power to our generators, and we can start saving money right now. We can also close the staff restaurant and get all the food and drink delivered to employees by the tubes. Another eight million saved. As an employee benefit, we can get access to generous tax breaks. Another twenty-four million saved a year. I suggest we brand this place 'The Energy Hub'."

Mr Givememore remained silent and frantically tapped away on his pocket calculator. For what seemed a few long minutes, he froze in delighted delirium before bouncing down from the rostrum and hugging Robert. He was almost dancing in delight as he thought of the increased DiaboliCo profits and bigger bonus payments this would get him.

"That's it, my boy! Genius! What a brilliant business mind you have! Jeez, you remind me so much of my younger self! Quite beautiful, a building powered by its own employees. We must patent the idea before anyone else. We can then make even more money from selling this idea to every other company in the world. Imagine it, Karma – every global employee working on their own personal treadwheel. Maybe we can get them in schools as well? Oh my, the world can get more and more productive, generating their own electricity and reducing obesity as well. It's quite brilliant! The shareholders will just love this! I'm going up to tell them now, watch the share price rocket!"

Mr Givememore skipped over to the elevator as he called out, "The Energy Hub – I love it, Karma! No doubt in my mind, you are now ready for a promotion to Vice President level. Getting really high now! Look out for the letter!"

26

The Rescue Mission

Velia Rose lowered a thick black hoodie over UMA's raised arms and wriggled the garment so that the robot's large round head could squeeze through the neck opening. His metal head eventually popped through, and his eyes instantly glowed with a bright yellow pulse of relief. Velia Rose lifted the hood so it covered UMA's head and nodded to herself. It should provide sufficient disguise. UMA nodded back at Velia Rose as she gave him a thumbs up, his rounded heart light flickering with a flashing red pulse.

The last few days had been awful, and while everyone was distracted with having to plan Dennis Baccino's funeral, everything still felt very unreal. Many people had called by the house to extend their sympathies to the family, and both Velia Rose and UMA had been happy making drinks and snacks for all of the sad and solemn visitors. UMA listened to many of the older guests, who reflected on Dennis's life, and the little robot observed that no one had ever mentioned his working life. Dennis had worked in the local toothpaste factory for thirty-eight years and skilfully painted the blue-and-red stripes on to the toothpaste.

UMA also observed the guests never even discussed any of the material possessions Dennis had acquired during his lifetime. He realised that people only wanted to remember the good times and talk about the life experiences they had shared with Dennis. UMA had learned that the real value of a person's life could only be adequately measured by the emotional impact they had made to others. The little robot understood that only humans had the unique capacity for love. It was the one thing that made them truly human.

It was now 8 p.m, and Lilly Baccino was tired and feeling a bit down, so had decided to have an early night. Velia Rose felt helpless, and thought her grandmother looked completely lost.

It was UMA who had presented a diagram to Velia Rose just a few hours earlier. The small robot had scribbled it on the painting easel that stood on the porch of the summer house. Velia Rose studied the diagram and immediately understood what UMA was trying to suggest to her. It was a rescue mission, which involved both her and UMA assuming the role of secret agents. The mission objective was simple: rescue Robert Karma from the city and return him to the Baccino garden. Once Robert understood what had happened to Dennis, he would realise that they all needed to be together again. They could then help each other heal and try to be happy again. It all sounded so simple.

The mission would not be easy, and it did present a few significant challenges that Velia Rose had contemplated and methodically scribbled down on her sketchbook paper.

Rescue mission action plan -

1. Issue - I have not left this house / garden in years.
Solution - get over myself, this is much more important!
2. Issue - a Robot will attract too much attention in the dangerous city.
Solution - wear disguise (me...cap / UMA old black hoodie top)
3. Issue - we still don't know where Robert is ?
Solution - UMA to research the inter-web to locate the target.
4. Issue - neither me or the robot talk!
Solution - hope people understand Makaton. If not...improvise.
5. Issue - need to get back home by midnight.
Solution - catch the 23:03 train from central city station.
6. Issue - I might get really hungry.
Solution - take an apple and 4 bags of crisps.

Velia Rose folded the action plan, placed it in her jeans pocket, and approached UMA, who was now sitting with the laptop rested on his bent metal knees. He could type remarkably fast, and she peeked over his shoulder as he tapped rapidly away on the keyboard. She looked at the screen as it streamed through hundreds of different screenshots, making it impossible for any human to digest so much information in such a short display time. However, UMA was a talented robot with a remarkable processing capability, and he continued to consume massive amounts of information. After eight minutes, he stood up and brought the laptop to Velia Rose, who was now fastening her coat and checking the contents of her small rucksack she had just packed for the mission.

The little robot had done well, as on the screen was a full

profile of Robert Karma. It was unbelievable how much stuff could be extracted about someone on the Internet, and UMA had collected information from various social media and online resources.

Amazingly, UMA had even found a way to access Robert's personal calendar, and they both scanned his busy schedule to identify his plans and whereabouts for that very evening.

Calendar

Karma, Robert

Tuesday ecember		Wednesday 8th December	Thursc 9th De
	06:00	Morning briefing with Mr Givememore	06:00
	07:00	Brainstorming session - headcount reduction	07:00
	08:00		08:00
	09:00	1 hour session in The Energy Hub (order new TV)	09:00
	10:00	Investigate global flip chart shortage issues	10:00
	11:00		11:00
	12:00	Profit analysis with Mr Givememore	12:00
	13:00	Meet with Human Resources - Downsizing push	13:00
	14:00		14:00
	15:00	Project Karoshi - phase 6 progress review	15:00
	16:00	Meet with Finance - Q4 budget review	16:00
	17:00	1 hour session in The Energy Hub (order new suits)	17:00
	18:00	Project Karoshi - phase 7 planning exercise	18:00
	19:00	Performance review with Mr Givememore	19:00
	20:00	Meet with Marketing - flip chart shortage complaint	20:00
	21:00	Company Networking Event (formal dress)	21:00
	22:00	The Stinky Kipper (111268 Austins Place)	22:00
	23:00	** 1st date with Chantelle **	23:00
	00:00	Submit end of day update report to Mr Givememore	00:00

Velia Rose patted UMA on the shoulder and gave him another thumbs up in recognition for the robot's superb investigative skills. She then held her finger to her lips to indicate they needed to be soundless as they left the garden. UMA nodded in agreement. It was time to leave the garden and catch the next train into the city, and Velia Rose grabbed her baseball cap and rucksack.

They needed to head for The Stinky Kipper.

27

Promotion Letter

DiaboliCo
WE REALLY GET YOU

FAO: Robert Karma (Level 162)
Employee number: 265533663663888883113

Dear Mr. Karma

We understand that you are about to gain career promotion to
Vice President level within DiaboliCo. Congratulations on
such a quick and impressive advancement!

In line with your signed contract of employment (clause 992,
section 12.1.b.ii), you will recall that all employees who reach
Vice President level require a mandatory simple surgical
procedure. This is standard contractual protocol at DiaboliCo,
and we remind you that this aspect of employment must be
treated as **strictly confidential**. Any breach of this
confidentiality will result in instant dismissal and certain
legal action, which may possibly destroy your life.

Please report to the Company Medical Unit (Level 129) at
4pm on Friday 9th December and ask for Doctor Pillager. The
procedure will take approximately 7 minutes, allowing you to
return to your workstation by 4:08pm.

DiaboliCo accept no liability for any adverse side effects you
may experience as a result of this contractual procedure.

Never forget, at DiaboliCo, we really get you! ©

Will Pillager

Dr. Pillager (Corporate Neurologist)
DiaboliCo Medical Unit (Level 129, DiaboliCo Tower)

28
The Stinky Kipper

Velia Rose and UMA boarded the train that would take them into the city. She had tucked her long dark hair under a large peaked red baseball cap, which helped to hide her beautiful face as she kept her head lowered while she sat next to her robotic travelling companion. Her heart was beating fast and hard, and although she was worried about what could go wrong with the rescue mission, she also felt giddy with excitement that she was making an adventure into the city and breaking away from the safe and tranquil garden.

UMA sat next to her, the large black hoodie covering his head and his upper half. His short metallic legs had been exposed, but he had dealt with this by pulling his legs up and hiding them under the chest area of the loose-fitting hoodie. The night train rumbled along the track into the city, and both UMA and Velia Rose could see the glowing dome of the city lights, like a large pale blue sphere that surrounded the large tower blocks that rose high into the night sky.

"Tickets, please! Tickets, please!" announced a fat ticket inspector who had just entered the carriage through a connecting door. The carriage was not very busy, and it wouldn't take the ticket inspector long to reach Velia Rose and UMA.

Velia Rose peeked a look at UMA and once again raised her finger to her mouth to signal that he should remain still and silent. UMA shrugged and kept his hooded head down as the inspector reached them. The fat ticket inspector looked down at them both and shook his head with disapproval.

"Feet down off the seats please, sir. Tickets for inspection," he said in a robotic monotone voice, as if he had said the same sentence a million times before.

Velia Rose reached for her train tickets, which were in her coat pocket, and UMA slowly slid his metal legs from under the hoodie and down from the seat, keeping his head lowered as he did so. The ticket inspector took the tickets from Velia Rose and quickly clipped them with his small metal clipper device. Just as he was about to return the tickets, he hesitated as he noticed the robot's small metal legs dangling from the train seat. The ticket inspector raised his eyebrows and seemed to freeze in deliberation. After what seemed an agonising few moments, he smiled at Velia Rose as he returned the tickets to her before moving on to the next   set of passengers further down the carriage. Velia Rose let out a sigh of relief and smiled at UMA, his yellow lens eyes projecting a bright beam like a lighthouse from inside his hood. *Life outside the garden wasn't so bad,* she thought, as a train carriage speaker announced that the next stop was where they would then need to change trains.

They were now in the city – well, actually, underneath the city. They stood on the platform of the underground tube station and awaited the next train, which would take them deeper into the city and to Austin's Place Station. A train approached from the dark tunnel, and a strong warm wind blew down the platform as the train rumbled into view. Velia Rose and UMA looked into the train as it started to slow to a stop and noticed that every carriage was jam-packed with people. Every seat was already taken, and people were standing uncomfortably close to each other, holding on to hanging loop straps that were dangling from the carriage ceiling. The train stopped and the door opened in front of Velia Rose and UMA. No one chose to get off the train, and all of the passengers standing in the doorway looked down coldly at Velia Rose and UMA as they stepped into the carriage.

The brave rescuers squeezed themselves into the squashed, thick wall of commuters. The train door closed, and they quickly scuttled through a labyrinth of dark underground tunnels. Velia Rose quietly observed the other passengers from beneath the peak of her baseball cap. She noticed that absolutely no one was smiling. No one was talking. Everyone in the carriage was alone and consumed by the electronic device they held in their agitated hands. Velia Rose had recently read all about mobile phone and technology addiction problems, and as she looked at everyone in the carriage totally absorbed with whatever information glared up at them, she understood she was now surrounded by technology addicts. After a few minutes, she raised her head and removed her baseball cap. None of the other passengers even looked up from their devices. Velia Rose then looked across at UMA, and quickly tugged at the back of his hoodie, pulling the hood down to reveal his perfectly rounded metal head. The little robot was surprised and reached to hold on to Velia Rose's arm.

She giggled as she pointed to all of the other passengers, so consumed on their personal devices that they didn't even realise they were sharing a train carriage with an incredible robot. UMA's heart light glowed bright red under his black hoodie as Velia Rose pointed around at the other passengers and impersonated a zombie.

UMA understood the joke. She was completely right; these people were just like the walking dead, looking low on human spirit and hypnotised by their precious and expensive electronic devices.

They exited the train, and along with seemingly hundreds of trance-induced commuters, moved through the station like they were being washed along in a strong river current. They turned a corner and could see they were approaching six large stainless steel escalators. Three of the escalators were moving a thick mass of commuters up into the city, while three of the escalators brought a continuous stream of passengers down into the underground station. It was so busy and congested in the city that it was not possible to even see the ground that you walked on.

Their natural instinct was to move along with the crowd – to go with the flow and move with the overwhelming current of the commuter river. Any resistance would be difficult and require great strength and perseverance. They joined the escalator and slowly moved up towards the city. Once again, Velia Rose noticed that everyone looked very serious or exhausted – or both. *No-one smiled.* UMA had remembered watching thousands of Yamanuchi robots working in the Chinese car factories. The tube station escalators crammed full of commuters reminded him of the car factory robots, thousands of identical robots all stood in organised lines, busy complying within a big efficient machine.

They stepped out from the tube station and into a cold, drizzly night in the city. Velia Rose retrieved her rescue mission action plan from her pocket and turned the paper over to get reacquainted with the street map she had jotted down. She quickly found her bearings and took UMA's hand as they headed towards The Stinky Kipper restaurant. It was the only ten-star gourmet restaurant in the world, and it was very exclusive and incredibly expensive. As they made their way through the busy streets, they noticed many people huddled on the wet pavements or hiding in dark alleyways. Velia Rose had never seen homeless people before and was amazed to see that they co-existed on the same streets as the busy, yet very affluent, city workers. She stopped and gave her apple and a packet of crisps to a young woman who lay on a cardboard mat. The girl looked surprised and thankfully accepted the food donation.

Velia Rose felt suddenly sad that this person had got lost in life, and had found herself alone on the bleak, uncaring city streets. *Anyone could get lost in modern life*, she thought, as they turned a corner and could see the luminous pale pink neon sign that dazzled above the restaurant's entrance.

She and UMA waited to cross the busy road, and UMA noticed that almost every car driver was trying to drive and use a mobile device at the same time. He shook his head in despair as a large black truck bumped into the rear of a small car, which in turn then knocked over a cyclist. The driver of the truck had been watching a movie on his laptop in the truck's cabin. *Maybe people were addicted to technology*, thought UMA, as he took Velia Rose's hand while they waited to cross the busy street.

A small group of paparazzi loitered outside the entrance, cameras hanging around their necks, as they stood like a family of hungry vultures, waiting for the next photo opportunity of some celebrity entering or leaving the lavish restaurant. Depending on the celebrity's popularity, the paparazzi would sometimes be allowed into the restaurant to quickly snap away at some willing fame-hungry superstar who wanted people to see them eating in such a nice and expensive place.

UMA thought quickly and pulled Velia Rose across the street and close to the paparazzi group. Suddenly, a large chunky black SUV with tinted windows parked up outside the restaurant entrance. The paparazzi jostled into action, as they already knew from looking at the vehicle that some celebrity was about to jump from the car and into the restaurant. The group of paparazzi moved closer to the car and had already starting clicking and flashing the cameras. A large bodyguard in a tight black suit quickly got out from the front passenger door and opened another sliding door at the side of the vehicle to reveal a small blonde woman dressed in a bright, tight-fitting sparkling gold dress, sitting beside a skinny little old man dressed in a dinner suit. The heavy wooden doors of the restaurant opened as a nervous-looking doorman held the door open, waiting for the celebrity couple to enter the restaurant quickly. The restaurant doorman watched impatiently as the little woman stepped out of the car and happily posed for the waiting paparazzi, proudly exhibiting her latest cosmetically enhanced face and body while she professionally turned her head quickly to allow her long blonde hair to swish and swirl around her aged boyfriend.

The waiting doorman eventually lost his patience as he stood at the restaurant door and sprang forward to the posing celebrity couple, in an attempt to usher them into the restaurant and away from the papping paparazzi. UMA spotted this tiny moment of opportunity, and quickly pulled Velia Rose through the unguarded entrance while the restaurant doorman got involved in a scuffle with the paparazzi and the burly bodyguard.

The robot closed the thick and heavy restaurant door behind them, and immediately it silenced the fracas that was occurring outside the restaurant. They had to think very quickly as a tall, imposing skinny man approached them in the candlelit lobby of the restaurant. The man was wearing a golden name badge that identified him as Philippe LaDiDa, Director of Guest Relations.

He smiled as he opened his stick-like arms to welcome his new guests. "Welcome, Duke and Duchess of Trumpington. Welcome to The Stinky Kipper. Please, let me take your coats and take you through to your table!"

Velia Rose looked up at Philippe from under her red baseball cap and nodded politely while she tightly squeezed UMA's small metal hand. Velia Rose could sense Philippe inspecting the very informal clothes that his new guests were wearing, and just as Velia Rose expected him to realise that they were not really VIP guests, Philippe suddenly gushed, "Our normal dress code is strictly formal attire, but of course, we understand that many of our royal guests have to dress down to avoid the attention of the horrible media people. Just last week the Queen herself dined here wearing a pink tracksuit and gangster shades. Very street! A most resourceful lady. Please, do follow me. We are truly honoured with your presence!"

Velia Rose and the little robot in the black hoodie quickly followed Philippe into the plush, luxurious dining area. Philippe smiled with pride as he led what he thought were two members of the royal family to the very best table in the house. The table was perched on a raised platform, which looked down on all of the other diners. Many of the diners stopped eating and stared in confounded silence as the girl in a baseball cap and a small hooded figure took their seats at the top table.

ſpecial ſervice Award

William Tickleschwing Snr sat alone in his office on level -19. It had been a long day, and he felt exhausted as he opened a new email that he had just received from the Human Resources department. He was already feeling empty inside when he read the message.

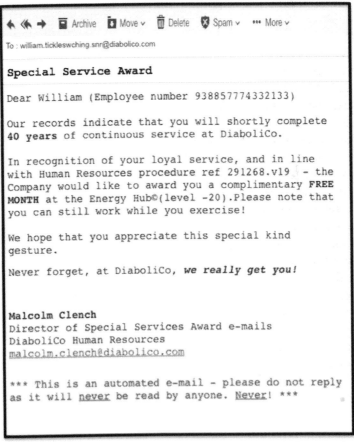

He was already grinding his teeth as he deleted the email, and he looked up at the wall monitors, which seemed to be continually beeping alerts of flip chart problems in every DiaboliCo global location. Since Billy Jnr had been terminated from the company, everything was going wrong. Billy Jnr had developed the sophisticated computer program that made the global flip chart system work so well. If anything went wrong, Billy Jnr could always fix it in a few minutes by altering or updating the code. The trouble was that Billy Jnr was no longer around, and William really missed his son. He knew how to use the system, but he had no idea of how to fix it if it broke. And it was really broken.

For the first time in almost forty years, DiaboliCo had experienced major supply outages of flip charts. William felt deeply distressed about this and knew that thousands of DiaboliCo employee meetings would not be able to use flip charts. He thought of all the brilliant brainstorming ideas that could now be lost if a flip chart was unavailable in important meetings. Thousands of DiaboliCo colleagues enjoyed flip charts for recording actions and issues. Many managers would now feel lost if they could not scribble complex diagrams and arrows on flip charts to share with their teams.

William Tickleschwing Snr looked at the map of the world that the computer monitor displayed. Every DiaboliCo location was represented by a flashing red dot, indicating a flip chart outage. There were more than 6,000 small flashing red dots flashing and bleeping on the map. It couldn't get any worse.

The bleeps continued as William Tickleschwing Snr emptied the contents of his desk drawer into a small brown cardboard box. He removed the poster from the wall, which had provided the illusion of a window frame looking out on to a sun-drenched beach touching a bright blue tropical ocean. The space where the poster was displayed now revealed a rectangle of un-faded grey concrete, reminding him that he stood in a man-made corporate tomb. He rolled the poster up and placed it in his cardboard box. Forty years' service, forty years of being buried nineteen floors below the city streets. Forty years of staying in the green. Forty years of being defined by a job that he was about to lose.

William Tickleschwing Snr stood at his office door for one last time and looked down at his security pass. Sure enough, its green light stopped flashing, and the expected red light then started to blink slowly. He carried his stuff to the elevator, thinking how it was possible to fit forty years of service into a small cheap cardboard box, and knowing that within the next minute a DiaboliCo security guard would be coming to swiftly escort him from the building.

30

Respected, Rejected, Ejected

Velia Rose smiled across the table at UMA, whose head was still covered in his black hoodie while his yellow eyes subtly glowed like distant lights from within the dark hole of the hoodie. She felt alive, and she loved this adventure in the city. They both realised they wouldn't have much time remaining in the restaurant, as they already could feel most of the diners staring and whisper about the two unusual customers. Unexpectedly, everyone in the room suddenly stood, and every person then looked directly at them. UMA felt very uneasy and was about to jump and run when Velia Rose made a few Makaton signs to the robot. *Stay calm. Stay sitting. This is fantastic fun! Enjoy the experience.*

Indeed, the fun very much continued as Philippe then publicly announced the arrival of the Duke and Duchess of Trumpington, before the familiar sounds of the British National Anthem filled the dining room. All the now-standing diners and restaurant staff pompously sang along as the two accidental dignitaries remained at the top table, nodding along to the loyal singing servants and impersonating the best royal wave they could improvise. The anthem finished, and the crowd cheered with rapture before returning to their seats to continue dining. Velia Rose shook her head in disbelief as UMA spoke to her in Makaton signs. *We need to find Robert. He is not in this room Let's look around. Let's go now!*

Velia Rose stood and quickly followed UMA as he made his way to an exit that lead to a staircase, which went upstairs. As they moved through the crowd, all of the diners smiled and nodded, and two passing elderly ladies even stopped to provide a curtsey. They reached the stairs and started to climb them when Velia Rose looked back across the dining room to the restaurant entrance. She quickened her speed when she realised that the doorman and the celebrity couple had now managed to enter the restaurant. They stood gesticulating and bickering with Philippe, who now looked highly embarrassed and flustered that he may have admitted the wrong VIPs into the swanky restaurant. Velia Rose knew they had very little time remaining in the restaurant as Philippe clicked his fingers and hastily summoned three waiters, pointing them in her direction.

UMA was now running along a dark corridor and could feel the thick red carpets beneath his metal feet. Velia Rose joined the robot as they reached a closed old antique style door, which boasted a brass nameplate, reading:

The Dahl Suite
Private Dining Room – DiaboliCo Executives Only

They didn't have time to plan, so Velia Rose promptly turned the door handle and pushed the door open. They entered the room; a raucous party was already well under way. People were drinking and laughing, and one drunken couple were even singing and dancing on a dining table as a bawdy group cheered and clapped. The room was very crowded and noisy as they scanned the room, looking for their lost friend. It was UMA who spotted Robert, sitting at a busy table on the far side of the chamber. The robot motioned to Velia Rose, and they both moved towards Robert, who was sitting with a large extravagant cocktail drink before him with one arm around a satisfied-looking Chantelle Golddigger, his other arm outstretched holding a fat, smouldering cigar. A group of fawning colleagues all sat around Robert, all smiling and sniggering as he finished his latest boast.

"This employee was practically *begging* me not to terminate him. The fool didn't realise he was number 100 this week! He had to go, or I wouldn't make my weekly termination target! Even old Givememore thought it was tough terminating someone just for being bald! Got my bonus, though!"

The group all howled with laughter as Robert sat centre-stage, smiling as he absorbed the accolades from his fellow executives. His smile quickly disappeared when he looked at the end of the table. The rowdy group that surrounded him turned to examine the two figures who stood silently, staring at Robert.

UMA removed the black hoodie to reveal himself fully, his circular heart light now pounding with a red pulsing glow. Velia Rose removed her baseball cap and her tussled black hair fell below her shoulders. Robert froze as the group around him went into a stunned mute mode. He maintained a serious expression as he asked abruptly, "Can I help you?".

Velia Rose reached for her rucksack and unzipped a side pocket, removing her drawing and pushing it on to the table surface so that it glided along the table to stop at the side of Robert's cocktail drink. He looked down at the pencil lifelike drawing, instantly recognising the image of the old man.

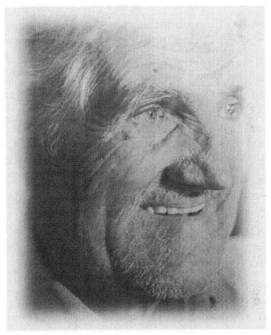

Robert looked at Velia Rose and shrugged. "Old Mr Baccino. Nice guy. Nice drawing, Velia Rose. How's the old man doing?" he asked as he took a sip from his cocktail drink.

Velia Rose shook her head slowly while UMA's heart light now glared with a cold, pale blue shine, and the little robot raised both of his metal hands in an attempt to cover its chest.

The chasing waiters had now arrived at the private dining room and were moving close to the two VIP imposters. Velia Rose suddenly wondered why she had ever left the garden. Robert felt like a stranger to her and she now felt very lost. She felt empty inside, and it felt very wrong being in this place. She took one last hard look at her friend as he sighed and then continued, "Sorry to hear about that. That's a tough break. But that's the past, and you can't move forward in life if you keep looking in the rear-view mirror."

Robert tossed the drawing of the old man back down along the table towards Velia Rose, but it failed to find its intended target as it spun off the table and then on to the floor. UMA was about to pick it up, but both the robot and Velia Rose were already being pulled away from Robert's table by the waiters and swiftly ejected from the restaurant.

Velia Rose kept her scream of pain inside as tears welled behind her closed eyes. UMA just didn't understand what had happened. Chantelle smirked and kissed Robert on the cheek, giggling. "Well, that was weird! Who were they? Someone you know?"

Robert shook his head as he sucked at the fat cigar, not really knowing who he was any more. He thought he had everything, but still, he felt empty inside. People fawned over him, and the party rolled on as Robert sat surrounded by business executives, celebrating wealth and business success.

He dropped his head to check for new emails on the handheld device that he held below table level. He began to respond to eight emails and quickly created three new meetings to drive more business profits.

In that moment, Robert Karma realised that *he* had become the Loneliest Robot.

31
A Simple Procedure

DIABOLICO
WE REALLY GET YOU

Robert stepped out from the elevator on level 129 and followed the signage leading him to the Medical Unit. He entered through the frosted-glass door and approached the large, severe-looking lady who sat behind the reception desk. He provided his appointment and employee details and the receptionist lightly tapped them into a computer keyboard. While she was doing this, Robert noticed a pleasant floral scent and followed it along the reception desk to find a little silver watering can that stood next to a plant pot, which housed a friendly bunch of red carnations. He smiled and thanked the receptionist after she instructed him to take a seat in the adjoining waiting room.

The waiting room also smelled very pleasant and oddly familiar as Robert took a seat on one of the few sofas that surrounded a coffee table. He leant forward to browse the several magazines that lay stacked on the table. Robert pulled a random magazine from the pile and was a little surprised to see that it was a copy of *Canal Barge Monthly*. Its cover featured several impressive canal barges, all of them featuring a smiling and waving passenger stood at the barge helm. Robert decided to take a look at the other magazine covers and was again a bit surprised to find *Gardeners' World*, *Italian Home Cooking* and a back copy of *Music Maker*.

He looked up and around the waiting room as some familiar music played out through a white ceiling speaker grill. The music featured a single piano, playing a melancholic and familiar piece that he couldn't quite recall the exact origin of. Over the delicate and elegant melody, he could hear the muffled sounds of two men discussing something from behind the door. The door carried the nameplate of Dr W. Pillager. Robert looked over to the corner, and on a small wooden table was a large glass jar containing some sort of brown powder. It stood next to a shiny letterbox-red teapot. Robert then recalled the pleasant smell in the waiting room that greeted him when he had entered. It was hot milky cocoa. A drink he had always enjoyed as a child. He walked to the corner and lifted the jar lid to smell the fine cocoa powder. He closed his eyes as he lowered his nose into the jar and took a deep sniff. It smelled so good.

He glanced around the room and now noticed several framed paintings that hung on each wall. A few of the works were awesome black and white line drawings, and the two other works featured bright, vivid, lush colours. He was just about to inspect them more carefully when the doctor's door opened, and Robert watched as an old man in a business suit was slowly led to the sofa area by Dr Pillager, who was wearing thick-rimmed spectacles along with the typical white lab coat.

The doctor noticed Robert standing in the corner, and smiled as he called over. "Ah, you must be young Mr Karma, here for your procedure. I'm just finishing up with Mr Pang and will need a few minutes to get things set up. Please relax and take a seat here with Mr Pang while he takes a little rest."

Dr Pillager patted the old man on the shoulder before adding, "Best of luck, old boy. Still life in the old dog yet I expect! Things will seem quite strange for a while, but it'll improve. You just need to find yourself again." The doctor then turned and briskly strolled into his office and closed the door behind him.

Robert sat next to Mr Pang, who was crouched forward on the sofa, holding his head down low as he rubbed and gently pinched the bridge of his nose with his old wrinkled fingers. The old man sighed and remained in this position as he opened up a conversation with Robert.

"Never thought this day would come. Been with DiaboliCo for forty-two years. Amazing how things flash by and before you know it, it's time to retire. I just had my extraction procedure, and the thing is, I can't seem to remember much about the last forty-two years."

The old man looked up from his crouched position, still kneading the bridge of his nose. Robert smiled and nodded, noticing Mr Pang had a pair of old thick-rimmed glasses dangling in the breast pocket of his white cotton shirt, and allowed the older man to continue.

"'Course, you're new. Young and fresh . . . it's all in front of you, boy. I was like you too – a bright, young, ambitious thing. Maybe I wanted it too much? I can't recall, being honest. It's all been a blur. I think I can remember my family, but they say my memories will slowly come back. I hope so . . . at least I should have enough money to enjoy my retirement. *Now I'm running out of time, not money.*"

Mr Pang chuckled and sighed to himself, while Robert felt a mix of confusion and concern. He chose to remain silent and politely smile as he waited to be called in by the doctor.

"Thing is, son, I don't *know* who I am any more. That extraction job has changed my thinking. They say things will come back to me slowly..." Mr Pang produced an unconvincing smile as he slowly massaged the bridge of his nose. A look of regret crossed the old man's face as the silence of the waiting room was broken.

"Ready for you now, Mr Karma, please come through." Dr Pillager now called as he stood at the open door of his examination room.

***

Robert entered the doctor's examination room and immediately noticed the reclining seat that stood alone in the centre of the room. The big chair was leather-covered and had a heavyset silver footrest at its base. A ceiling-mounted examination light hung down above the old seat and surrounding it was a small mobile stainless steel trolley that contained various compartments which stored medical devices and utensils. In the far corner of the room was an examination table that stood next to tall, white, portable privacy curtains.

Dr Pillager closed the door behind him and joined Robert, who was looking around the room at various items that looked somehow misplaced in a doctor's office.

"Excuse the mess in here, Mr Karma. Just had the decorators in. Still a load of weird junk in here that they need to remove. Now, please take a seat. This won't take too long."

Robert sat down in the old leather-backed chair and remained sitting upright as the doctor ran through a quick checklist of medical questions. He answered the questions as he looked around the room, feeling intrigued and slightly puzzled. He looked at the doctor's desk and studied the small bronze fisherman statue. The lone statue figure was standing at a ship's wheel staring out into the distance, as if he was searching for something – or someone. Beside the statue stood a small model of a lighthouse.

The doctor continued to fill in some legal documentation as Robert looked at a violin that was hanging on the wall behind the physician's desk. Next to the violin was a hanging framed lifelike drawing of an old-style vintage gramophone. Robert now felt a little uneasy as his chair began to slowly recline and Dr Pillager's grinning face came into view. It hovered above Robert's own face as he lay horizontally on the now fully reclined chair. Robert could see the reflection of his own face in the thick glass lenses of the doctor's spectacles. He didn't like what he saw in his reflection. Was that really himself that he could see?

"As you know, Mr Karma, this procedure is entirely contractual and will only take a few minutes. You are kindly reminded that it is a strictly confidential matter. Is everything clear before we proceed?"

Robert felt compelled to nod and agree to everything, but he somehow resisted the urge and surprised the doctor by asking him a question. "What are you going to do to me? The old man in the waiting room, Mr Pang, he mentioned something about an extraction. What are you going to take from me?"

Dr Pillager looked down at his patient and laughed as he hovered closely above Robert's face. "Extraction? Extraction! Now, that's a good one. Haha! Extractions are for the people we are finished with, Mr Karma! You are here for an *implant*. Surely you realise this?"

Robert felt numb and perplexed as the doctor's attention switched to his apparatus, and he started assembling some sort of medical utensil that Robert could not see.

"Implant of what?" asked Robert.

The doctor smiled as he looked down at Robert again, then slowly removed his thick black-rimmed glasses to reveal a small rectangle input port that was located in the centre of the bridge of his nose, right between his eyes. A little blue light flashed in the middle of a large implanted microchip.

"Why, the DiaboliCo EC4000 chip, Mr Karma! Much better than our previous executive control chips. It will multiply your processing capability by 4000 and allow management remote control access to ensure all company objectives are being efficiently delivered. You will operate much more efficiently. You will get so much more done and make much more money than you could ever need!"

"These new blue chipsets are quite remarkable, and they even remove any trace of emotional feelings or empathy so that every business decision is entirely financial. The only minor downside is the loss of personal memory, but since you are so young, you won't have any memories of any real value to worry about. Now please, let us proceed."

Robert lay fully back and looked up as the doctor angled the examination light so it shone directly into his face. The doctor switched on a small whirring medical device and moved his shoulder as he reached across to the apparatus, his movement revealing a painting, which was fastened to the ceiling right above Robert. He recognised the picture – it was the Baccino garden in beautiful lush colours, featuring the big tall Baccino house. He instantly remembered the round attic window that was perched at the top of the house. He remembered how many times he had looked up at that window with a sense that he was being watched.

Robert could now hear a small drilling sound, its humming noise moving closer as he stared deep at the painting again and far into the empty attic window. He felt the doctor moving closer. In the attic window, he suddenly spotted a small dark figure, waving out at Robert as if it were pleading or shouting. Robert's eyes were fixated on the painting as he struggled to focus on the figure in the window. Out of the corner of his eye, he could hear and see a silver drill head whirring speedily, now positioned just above the bridge of his nose. Robert took one last look into the attic window and then he saw her. She was now in clear view. It was the angelic face of Velia Rose, desperately calling out and banging both her fists on the attic window.

The doctor's shoulder moved above Robert's face and blocked his view of the captivating painting. The drilling screech sound grew louder as the doctor leant closely into his face.

"Now keep still, my friend, this won't hurt one bit. Never forget, son – at DiaboliCo, *we really get you.*"

32
Quiet in the Garden

The old barber's chair stood empty at the edge of the canal. It was now mid-winter, and most of the birds in the garden had now migrated to warmer climes. The garden was still and silent in its deep green hibernation, awaiting the spring to return its colour and life. Lilly Baccino wanted spring to come. She needed to feel the beginning of something new again. Life had to move on, but just now, it felt like it was frozen.

Velia Rose and UMA had been very quiet and distracted during the last week or so, and Lilly was worried about them. They spent most of the time in the summer house, and the old lady shrugged and smiled to herself as she thought maybe *she* was the one person she should worry about, sitting outside and alone on a chilly winter's day. It was cold, and the absence of music playing from the old gramophone made the garden feel detached in solitude. She stared at the empty barber's chair, warming herself inside with happy memories.

As was his usual daily routine, UMA scanned the laptop while Velia Rose slept in her bed. His small metal fingers diligently tapped away as he browsed many Chinese websites that contained old documents and many archive file images. His heart light would pulse a mix of blue and red glows as he explored a never-ending expanse of information, not yet finding what he searched for. After a few hours, the little robot flipped down the lid of the laptop, his heart light emitting a pale blue ball, and looked across to Velia Rose.

It had been painfully quiet in the summer house since they had returned from the failed rescue mission in the city. While it was very usual for Velia Rose to remain silent, she would usually be happily preoccupied with her art, reading, or music. In the last week, however, she had seemed lost and defeated. UMA had tried to gently encourage her to pick up a musical instrument or to return to a favourite book, but Velia Rose politely declined and chose to either reflect quietly or sleep when she was wasn't helping her grandmother around the quiet house. She just wanted to help her grandmother feel better but felt there was no obvious fix, other than allowing time to slowly pass in the hope it would help heal the deep pain of losing Dennis Baccino.

All at once, UMA had an idea, and he stood and moved quickly towards the small table in the summer house. He reached for one of the charcoal sketching pencils and began busily drawing and scribbling on some blank paper that lay on the table. Velia Rose looked over at the little robot engrossed in his activity, rubbing her eyes as she arose from the bed and walked over to observe his work. She reached UMA and placed her small pale hand on his shoulder as he continued to scrawl and jot. She looked down at his work and felt a mix of dread and hope. Her instinct was to turn and return to bed, shaking her head and thinking that the idea that UMA had would now be impossible. At that moment, though, she looked out at the canal and could see her grandmother sitting alone, next to the empty barber's chair, on the bank of the silent canal.

Velia Rose nodded to herself abruptly and promptly sat next to UMA. To the robot's relief, she smiled warmly as she pulled the paper over to herself. She continued the work that UMA had begun, before realising that they needed something vital if this project could succeed. She pointed to the door of the summer house. UMA understood her direction and was already on his feet, knowing his project task would not be easy.

After all, robots were not natural swimmers.

33

Project Haro∫hi - Project Wrap-Up ∫e∫∫ion

As usual, the bedside alarm clock awoke Robert at 04:30 a.m. He reached across to mute the alarm, halting the same song that woke him every day, and while his arm was outstretched, he collected his thick black-rimmed spectacles that lay on his bedside drawer. He then proceeded with his predictable morning routine, leaving his dreary small apartment that looked just like every other apartment in his block, before joining the same pack of commuters, sharing the clickety-clacking trance into the bowels of the dark, uncaring city. He had not had much sleep and was just as tired as all of the other exhausted-looking commuters.

He smiled to himself as he entered DiaboliCo Tower, wearing his new thick-rimmed spectacles, which felt quite comfortable and were much lighter than he had expected. During the journey, he sent several critical text messages to help finalise Project Karōshi. At 5:58 a.m., Robert entered the building and got into a waiting elevator, pressing the button for level -20. He wanted to visit The Energy Hub, hoping he could find Mr Givememore. The small, square, relentless CEO had recently got into the habit of visiting the hub at the beginning of each workday. He liked to monitor the amount of electrical kilowatts that his employees had generated in the previous twenty-four hours, and he especially enjoyed calculating how much money this had produced for the company. It would usually put him in a good mood before his first meeting of the day.

The elevator doors opened up on level -20 and Robert once again smiled as he recognised the familiar small figure now leaning forward (revealing a very square-shaped bottom) and inspecting the digital electrical meter that was located at the base of the closest treadwheel.

Robert moved closer and could hear Mr Givememore mutter as he took the meter reading. "Hmm, 4.4million megawatts generated in the last twenty-hours. Not bad, but I am sure these damned slackers could do more!"

Robert gently coughed to announce his arrival, and this triggered Mr Givememore to turn and look up. He looked at Robert and instantly gave a nod of admiration when he spotted the new thick-rimmed spectacles that now surrounded Robert's eyes. He beamed proudly as he returned to a standing position and looked up at his young and loyal prodigy.

"Oh, Karma! Oh, my boy! Just look at you! You really have arrived now at DiaboliCo. You are now one of us. Jeez, you remind me so much of my younger self! Welcome to the board of management. There is so much more we can do, so much more money to make!" he squawked, now sounding giddy.

Robert quietly nodded, looking around The Energy Hub and feeling satisfied that the many long rows of human treadwheels were currently empty and silent. He looked down calmly at his mobile device and selected an app that was titled DiaboliCo Building Services. The app opened up, and Robert quickly and expertly found the system that he wanted to control. He was then prompted to confirm his next command, and he privately did this while Mr Givememore started to jump up and down, waving his hands around.

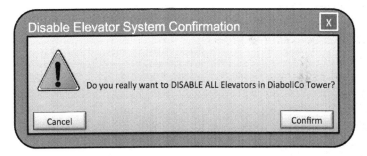

Robert turned to look at the elevators and quietly nodded to himself when the touch screen located above the call button was now displaying an "Out of Service" message. He returned his attention to Mr Givememore, who was still snapping away and gesticulating with both hands.

"I tell you, Karma, this lot can do better than this! We can generate much more energy if those ... *freeloaders* put some real effort in. The employees, *those slackers*, are just jogging on these things and plodding along with the work stuff! Imagine how much more we could make if we pushed them a bit more. The shareholders are demanding more profit, Karma. We need to show these employees how it's done! Get a productivity boost. It looks easy enough to me!" The CEO shook with agitation.

"Show me, sir," Robert replied. "You have been such a great mentor to me, could you show me how to take these things to the limit? We can even video it and share it with all global employees on a live worldwide broadcast. If the CEO can push it this hard, then all employees should too. It would be such a powerful message from the top, sir! I am sure we could generate 10 million megawatts a day. That's another 1.37% return to our shareholders. They would love you even more. Just imagine your cash bonus."

As Robert expected, Mr Givememore's face lit up at the very thought of increased profits and a bigger cash bonus. He puffed out his boxy square chest while silently nodding in agreement, thinking all the time of acquiring more wealth that he didn't need.

"Quite, Karma. Quite. Excellent input once again. Jeez, you remind me so much of my younger self! Let's do this thing!" Mr Givememore trotted quickly over to the nearest treadwheel on his stubby little legs. He then jumped inside the caged metal wheel. "I'll show those slackers how it's done, Karma! You ready to start recording this?" he barked, as he stood within the treadwheel, pathetically starting to stretch like an Olympic athlete before a sprinting contest.

"Just one minute, sir!" Robert tapped to put his mobile device into video-recording mode. He then looked behind Mr Givememore's metal treadwheel and was relieved to see a figure step out from the dark shadows. Billy Tickleschwing Jnr stood there holding a laptop that was fully wired to the treadwheel control panel. He was wearing a wide and reassuring smile as he gave Robert a silent thumbs-up gesture.

Mr Givememore gave a few more little star jumps as he exhaled a few small breaths in readiness for his global demonstration. Robert returned a silent thumbs-up gesture to Billy Jnr, still out of sight from Mr Givememore, and started the video recording as he pointed the camera at Mr Givememore. Robert smiled at the square little man, who looked quite ridiculous on the treadwheel.

"You are now live to the global employee base, sir! Over 400,000 employees! Good luck, sir!" Robert called.

Mr Givememore stared into the camera and a calm and authentic-looking smile settled on his face as he greeted his global employee audience. He spoke with a false kindness in his voice and offered words that subtlety implied job insecurity and fear to the watching masses, before providing a friendly smile and a wink to the camera.

He then faced the treadwheel. "Remember everyone. At DiaboliCo, we must do more with less! Activate now!"

The treadwheel responded by groaning and clinking into movement. The heavy metal cage began to slowly turn and revolve as Mr Givememore provided a confident smile to the camera. As before, hydraulic metal arms sprang into life, moving around the turning treadwheel and positioning a laptop in front of Mr Givememore, while a telephone headset was lowered on to his square head. A camera that was connected to another metal arm moved into position above him, slowly flashing a green light to indicate acceptable employee performance. The food and drink tubes were lowered like wet slimy snakes as they dangled by the side of Mr Givememore.

"Working at DiaboliCo has never been easier! Everything you need, conveniently placed around you, our valued employee, our most valuable asset!" said Mr Givememore as the wheel slowly accelerated and the laptop started making notification beeps.

"Watch me as I quickly take valuable personal exercise while I effortlessly work through email and work actions . . ." he continued, already starting to breathe heavily.

Robert smiled as he continued recording, nodding discreetly to Billy Jnr, who then began to tap complex code into the laptop keyboard that controlled the treadwheel and connected devices. Robert had found Billy Jnr the previous night, after he had searched several local refuges and hostels, eventually finding him at one of the city food banks.

They had worked through most of the night in planning this act of corporate revenge. Robert had sincerely apologised to Billy Jnr and explained what had happened to him at the company medical unit. Billy Jnr had not hesitated in agreeing to help out his old friend and colleague. He had unfinished business with DiaboliCo himself, after all.

The treadwheel was now whirring as it moved at a very steady pace; new emails arrived every four seconds and a queue of nine phone calls displayed on the laptop screen. At that point, Mr Givememore was invited to three different videoconferences. Not wanting to show any sign of weakness, he continued to smile at the camera through deep, heavy breaths ,and he prodded the laptop with his stubby fingers, joining three different video conference calls. Sweat was now running down his face as he plastered on a false smile while he greeted the other participants of the video conference calls.

"Hi, everyone! Let's see what we can achieve—" he broke off to wipe a trickle of sweat off his noise and gulp down mouthfuls of air "—today. At DiaboliCo we—" Mr Givememore coughed and spluttered and fought to regain control "—we really get you!"

Robert kept recording as he gestured to Mr Givememore to keep going, as Billy Jnr busily tapped away to generate more and more work for him. The laptop started to beep as every email was titled "Urgent! Response required now!". Mr Givememore looked up at the camera within the treadwheel, his face now straining further as he noticed the green flashing light turn to amber, indicating that his performance level required quick improvement. Robert felt the need to apply some added pressure to the cruel executive, and offered a suggestion to his boss, who was now panting like a wolfhound.

"Time to order food and drink, sir! What's on the menu today?"

Mr Givememore was now really struggling to keep up with the treadwheel as it continued to accelerate. But he knew he couldn't possibly show any sign of weakness, so produced a thin smile as he placed his order.

"Food order. Pea soup with liquidised bread. Drink order, extra strong coffee!" he gasped.

His small legs were now running at full capacity as he hopelessly tried to accomplish the many tasks that were demanded of him. Robert stepped closer to his frazzled boss, and as Mr Givememore quickly turned to face him, Robert removed his own thick-rimmed spectacles that he was wearing. Mr Givememore was completely breathless but was still able to see that Robert did not reveal the expected DiaboliCo EC4000 chip implant. He looked puzzled, then confused, and then looked infuriated as he realised Robert had not gone through with the required company procedure.

Mr Givememore was close to physical and mental collapse now, but still he valiantly – and stupidly – tried to keep up with the quickening pace of the turning large wheel and the multiple different work demands that increased in volume as he became more and more stressed. Sweat now dripped from his square head as a mist of condensation started to fill his own spectacles. Before the mist fully clouded his vision, he looked up and held his mouth open as the amber flashing light switched to a slow red blink. He looked at the camera monitor in exasperated dismay as he shook his disbelieving head. His spectacles then slipped away from his hot, clammy head, revealing a large chip implant fixed between his eyes.

The chip featured a small flashing blue light and Robert zoomed into a closer view with the video recorder.

It was at this point that Mr Givememore received his food and drink order, the putrid green pea soup squirting in his face, as hot and thick black espresso coffee spilled over his damp and sweaty white shirt. He was now totally humiliated and beginning to realise that pushing people too hard could have very bad consequences.

The treadwheel then suddenly stopped turning, and all of the devices that surrounded Mr Givememore were quickly withdrawn. The little man stood still as the unit made a deep disapproving beep followed by a computerised voice, which made an announcement. "Termination. Unacceptable performance. Error code 966. New recruitment request sent to human resources."

Mr Givememore knew what would happen next, and before he was expelled from the treadwheel, he locked his beady, raging eyes on to Robert. He was almost too exhausted to speak, but Robert could feel the hate and anger bubbling inside the dangerous little man as the blue light of his chip implant continued to flash. Robert almost felt a grain of sympathy for the exhausted executive as he shook his sweaty square head and sighed, "Jeez, and you reminded me so much of my younger self."

Robert smiled and moved closer to his beaten senior. "Don't ever forget, Mr Givememore. At DiaboliCo, we really get you!" he whispered.

At that moment, the metal grid below Mr Givememore opened, and a dark gaping hole swallowed up the evil business executive. The CEO squealed as he fell into a world of rejection that he had created himself. The grid closed with a solid clunk as Robert turned the camera towards his own face, knowing that a global audience of over 400,000 employees would be still captivated by the live employee broadcast.

Robert smiled and nodded before he addressed the global audience. "Yes, folks, that really happened. Believe what you just watched. The Chief Executive Officer and the whole upper board of management at DiaboliCo are greedy corporate robots. They are programmed to just make more money for the company, and will only ever think about the company, not you. That's all they care about. They will only ever want to get more with less. While you figure it out, watch this . . ."

Robert turned the camera back towards the long rows of empty treadwheels and nodded to Billy Jnr, who once again tapped passwords and more complex code into the laptop. Within seconds, one of the large hydraulic, mechanical arms reached up to the upper arch of the nearest treadwheel and pushed it on to its side with a mighty crash. As it fell, it created a domino effect, and all of the standing metal treadwheels started to topple into each other, each treadwheel taking another to the ground with a loud resounding smash. Row after row tumbled to the ground. After two minutes of loud, toppling crashes, the last treadwheel dropped to the ground.

Through the tinny laptop speakers, Robert and Billy Jnr could hear the global audience scream and cheer with grateful applause. Once again, Robert turned the camera on himself and a very satisfied-looking Billy Jnr. He was happy to conclude the broadcast.

"So, with that, I can officially announce that Project Karōshi is now terminated, and we will be happily breaching company confidentiality by reporting DiaboliCo to the appropriate authorities. You guys deserve a fair employer! That ends today's global employee broadcast, thanks for joining us today!"

Robert and Billy Jnr gleefully waved at the camera before Billy Jnr hollered with joy. "And never forget, at DiaboliCo, we really get . . . *even!*"

The global audience erupted once again into delirious whooping and cheering as Robert ended the broadcast. He looked across at Billy Jnr who was busy hacking into another DiaboliCo system. Robert smiled and felt a wave of pure release wash over him. He felt like he had awoken from a long, self-induced coma, and felt very close to being free from this place.

"Just two more minutes, mate. There's something I have to do to really even the score around here," Billy Jnr said, as he rapidly tapped away on the laptop.

Robert re-enabled the elevator system and pressed the button to summon a ride back up to ground level. He needed to get out from this concrete tomb and get some fresh, clean air. As he waited and watched Billy Jnr do his stuff, he thought about had happened in the company medical unit.

He recalled the unbelievable urge to push Dr Pillager away, not so much to stop the crazy chip implant procedure, but to allow himself to see if Velia Rose was still standing at her window, crying for help. Robert didn't realise he could feel so strongly about someone and instantly understood what really mattered to him. There were just a few things that really puzzled him about the doctor's waiting room and the examination room.

Robert entered the elevator and waited for his friend to join him as Billy Jnr flipped down the lid of the laptop and smiled across to Robert. As his friend approached the elevator, Robert's mind returned again to the company medical unit. All that random stuff in there had reminded him so much of the Baccino garden, the one place he could be truly happy. The one place he belonged. Was he so lost that he needed subliminal reminders of that special place in his heart? If so, how?

He then had the clearest recollection of what he had seen while he chaotically stumbled around to escape the doctor's treatment room. Robert remembered it all. It was so very clear in his mind, and now he understood completely. He replayed the scene in his mind once again, watching in slow motion as the surprised Dr Pillager fell back on to the floor. The floored and flustered doctor had a surgical drill held in one hand and a DiaboliCo microchip in the other, and as he fell he knocked a stainless steel trolley over. It slammed into the ground while the ceiling-mounted examination light swung around wildly above the hapless doctor.

Despite all of this commotion, Robert had somehow noticed the portable white privacy curtain that stood at the back of the room by the examination bed. Not that a white privacy curtain was particularly interesting to him then. But what caught his eye was a familiar red circular light glow that appeared from behind the curtain, shining through the thin cloth like summer sunlight radiates through a bedroom curtain. He smiled to himself as he recalled the two small metallic feet that stood at the base of the privacy curtain.

Billy Jnr joined him in the elevator, and they started their ascent within the tower. It was then that Robert giggled out loud as it occurred to him that mobile curtains move around on wheels, not on feet that resembled a certain robot friend.

34
Lost in the City

Robert and Billy Tickleschwing Jnr left DiaboliCo Towers and had a very busy day in the city. They both dealt with several television and newspaper interviews after they had spent the day formally reporting the business malpractice of DiaboliCo to the local business authorities. Now that they had exposed DiaboliCo, the two young men stood at the large window of an electrical appliance store. They were watching the many banks of large televisions screens broadcasting various images and messages. Most of the screens were running the early evening news and breaking the news of what had happened at DiaboliCo, accompanied by live film footage of hundreds of DiaboliCo business executives being lead out of DiaboliCo Towers by a chain of police officers.

All the business executives still wore their thick-rimmed spectacles to disguise the corporate microchip that was still controlling their minds, and they left the corporate tower with their heads held low. Robert smiled as he recognised Dr Pillager being led away by a senior-looking police officer. Sadly, most of the news reports seemed to focus on the 90% drop in DiaboliCo share price, as if the only damage from this whole episode was of a financial nature. *Maybe society was just as obsessed with money as the crazy robotic people who had controlled DiaboliCo?* Robert mused.

His attention then shifted to his jacket pocket, where his mobile phone buzzed and vibrated to signal that he had received a new message. He opened the message from Chantelle Golddigger and allowed Billy Jnr watch the text conversation evolve, both of them chuckling and shaking their heads as another cold hard evening in the city approached.

We are so OVER!

OK

Cant believe you threw it all away! You fool! You will regret this!

I'm fine. Good luck Chantelle.

Anyway, I found myself a new wealthy boyfriend who has his own private yacht! Please don't chase after me!

OK. Bye.

Robert had no intention of returning to his city apartment. It was a dull, small place that was a duplicate of a million other one-bedroom apartments in this uncaring city. Robert and Billy Jnr also knew it would just be a matter of hours before anything associated with DiaboliCo would be disabled. The company mobile phone, the company laptop and the company credit cards. Robert also knew that the DiaboliCo Payroll Department immediately notified the credit rating authorities and understood that the access key to his new rented apartment would already be de-activated once it was clear that he would no longer have any regular income to afford the rent. Robert now had nothing and he knew he needed to find alternative accommodation for the night.

Billy Jnr had already been staying at a night shelter in the city, but could not find a place for Robert at the same place as it was full. While they looked around, Robert was staggered by how many people in a wealthy city were poor and destitute. There was an economic underbelly of the city that was not reported by the media. He guessed it wasn't exciting enough and rather unpleasant, so could make the viewers switch the channel. The people who lived on the streets did not have access to televisions, newspapers, or social media. These people were too distracted by worrying about how they find food and shelter in a cold and heartless city. They tried several more shelters and refuges for the homeless, but again, they could not find a warm bed for the night, and Robert started to consider the very real option of having to sleep out on the streets.

They headed for an all-night soup kitchen, which was run by volunteers. They were cold and hungry and stood quietly in the busy queue as they slowly edged towards the small serving hatch, which emitted an inviting cloud of steaming soup. They eventually reached the serving area and were both flabbergasted as they held out the cold empty bowls towards the man serving from a large steaming soup pan.

"Dad?" Billy Tickleschwing Jnr asked warily.

William Tickleschwing Snr dropped his serving ladle and stood transfixed as he tried to comprehend that Billy Jnr and Robert now stood before him with outstretched bowls. The older man was still smartly dressed, but his business suit had started to look a bit ragged at the edges. His hair was ruffled and his thick-rimmed spectacles full of soup steam. The condensation soon lifted on the glass of his spectacles, revealing tired red eyes that were now full of tears.

After the Tickleschwings had warmly embraced – for they had been cut adrift from each other since being terminated from DiaboliCo – they found a corner of the makeshift dining hall and sat with Robert at a window table while they all enjoyed some warm, but flavourless, watery soup. William Tickleschwing Snr shifted uncomfortably in his seat and looked a little ashamed that his life had brought him to such a desperate place.

He cleared his throat, and with a frightened look, shared his real feelings about his son for the first time. "Billy Jnr, I am so happy you escaped from that company. I read about it all in the news today. I was so so wrong. I gave them my life. They even took my pension away. I was left with nothing. Forty years' service. What a waste! At least you won't do the same thing." The old man's shoulders slumped and his voice trembled.

Billy Jnr remained silent but provided a nod of empathy while Robert quickly interjected. "But Mr Tickleschwing, it's not totally your fault, they have been controlling your mind for all of these years! We just need to get the blue chip extracted, and you'll soon be fine."

William Tickleschwing Snr sighed as he reached for his thick-rimmed glasses, removing them slowly from his weary face. Robert looked carefully, but could not see any sign of a chip implant on the old man's face, just some red pinch marks from where the spectacles had rubbed against the cold bridge of his nose.

The old man sighed. "I know what you're thinking, boys, but you need to understand that I got brainwashed without the need for a chip implant. All I ever wanted to do was succeed at the company, and I hoped that my personal efforts would be eventually recognised. I did everything they wanted and gave them all my time, all my life, for the sake of a lousy career, never making it beyond flip charts!"

"The majority of working people in this city don't need a chip implant to control them. They are 90% robot already! Just look at them all! Promise them some money, and they will do the same thing, every single day, working harder and longer, while life quickly passes them by. Buy more. Work more. Buy more. Work more. Thats the never-ending cycle."

William Tickleschwing Snr was now looking full of regret as he reached out to hold Billy Jnr's hand. "I am sorry I was not a better father to you, son. I only ever wanted you to do well, and to be happy. I forced my career ambition on to you. I knew you had so much ability, but I pushed you into something that you didn't want, and you were right, son. I am so sorry. Follow your dreams from now on."

The three of them sat quietly at the table, reflecting on things for a few moments, before Billy Jnr tapped on the table and unexpectedly started whistling, prompting the full attention of the two people with whom he shared the small dinner table. William Tickleschwing Snr was entirely puzzled but smiled at his unpredictable son all the same. Robert sat patiently, seeing that Billy Jnr was sitting on some news to share.

"So, Robert," Billy Jnr began, "you haven't asked me yet."

"Asked you what?"

"What else did I manage to fix while we were playing around with DiaboliCo systems earlier today" Billy Jnr smirked as Robert now recalled how his friend had asked for more time to work away on his laptop before they left DiaboliCo Tower.

Robert shrugged but was intrigued.

"Well, let's just say that DiaboliCo has made a significant financial compensation payment to all employees who were unfairly terminated from the company. Just my way of squaring the circle, if we must use corporate talk." Billy Jnr held his grin as he watched Robert's surprised look.

"But they will detect any payment and reverse it!" Robert cried.

"Hacked." came the quick reply from Billy Jnr.

"They can trace all payments and will hunt you down!"

"Hacked!" Billy Jnr shouted, chuckling.

"But Billy, all the signed employee contracts with the company allow them to terminate people without payment" Robert pointed out.

"*Hacked!*" howled a now giggling Billy Jnr. "I created a self-destructible, non-traceable program that deleted all the previous employee contracts and replaced them with fair and equitable contracts. Quite smart, I think! I also made all payment trails invisible to DiaboliCo systems, so they cannot trace where the compensation payments went. Don't worry, my friend, it's well sorted. I could have taken more, but I just wanted fairness for the people who they rejected and shunned. It might just reduce the company profitability by 0.002%, though!"

After a few more minutes, Billy Jnr had convinced both Robert and his dad that what he had done was fair and justified. They looked around the soup kitchen and knew they had to do something to escape from this sad and unfortunate place. Once again, Billy Jnr lightly tapped on the table and began to whistle an annoying tune.

Robert chuckled and shook his head. "Okay, Billy. What now? What else have you got to share with us?"

It was now Billy Jnr's time to share how he actually felt, and he didn't disappoint his fellow listeners. "All my life, people have asked me what I wanted to be. They said I was smart, so I should be able to make a lot of money. Even school pushed me in that direction. No one ever asked me what made me *happy*. I only ever wanted to be happy. Everyone seems to equate wealth with happiness. They are two very different things...just look at Mr Givememore. He had a ridiculous amount of money. He had incredible power and enjoyed good health. He was the most successful businessperson in this city! Was he a happy person?"

Robert and William Tickleschwing Snr both shook their heads.

"Exactly! Everyone thinks that wealth equals success, but it doesn't. Happiness can only come if you follow your own path, not a path that someone else has built for you. Success doesn't make you happy, *but getting happy is success!*"

Billy Jnr allowed himself a short silence before looking to his father. "Gotta say, Dad, you seemed a natural when I saw you serving soup to all those people before. Much better, with all respect, than you were at controlling global flip chart supplies!"

His father was now bewildered, not knowing where this was going, or if he could follow.

Billy Jnr continued, "So, I thought that I could do with that type of skill set to help me out in the new place. We could invest our DiaboliCo compensation payments to excellent effect. I have already spotted a place out in the country, out of this dirty, cold city. We spent way too much time being buried alive, stuck underground on level -19. This next place gives us around-the-clock access to fresh air, daylight and real people! It's gonna be great, Dad. We can succeed on our own terms this time! No one to tell us what to do!"

His father looked intrigued but obviously wasn't quite sure what Billy was talking about. He shrugged and offered a blank expression to his son before the answer came flowing back at him.

"The Tickleschwing Bakery! I can see it all now, Dad! You at the front of shop, dealing with the folks. I would be in the back, creating wonderful things and chasing my dream to make beautiful stuff for people to enjoy. That's my bliss, and I'm going to chase it! You in with me?"

Billy Jnr didn't have to wait long for an answer. William Tickleschwing Snr promptly stood up, unfastened and removed the soup-stained apron that was hanging over his business suit, and gleefully discarded the formal grey silk tie that had almost throttled him for the last forty years. He smiled and instantly looked ten years younger as colour filled his face. He shook his son's hand before taking Robert's.

The old man looked Robert directly in the eye. "Thank you, Robert. I know you got yourself lost for a while as well, but the important thing is that you found yourself. There is always time to try to fix things."

William Tickleschwing Snr turned to his son, rubbing his cold hands in anticipation of better times ahead and beaming a broad and hopeful smile. "Come on, Billy, let's go and try to catch a night train out of this city. We've wasted enough time here already. The Tickleschwing Bakery awaits!"

Billy Jnr stood to join his father, but then paused as he stooped down to talk to Robert. "We could use some more help if you want to come along for the ride?" he asked with raised eyebrows.

Robert shrugged and raised his open hands as he slowly shook his head from side to side.

Billy Jnr thought he understood what was on Robert's mind. "You going to try to fix things in that garden place you always told me about?"

Robert shrugged again, reminding himself that he had been a fool. He feared he had burned his bridges with that particular place. The Tickleschwings embraced Robert and then left the busy soup kitchen and headed out into the dark city. Robert silently watched them cross the frosty road and out of his life. He felt happy for them, and his glad smile remained for minutes after they disappeared from his view.

Robert was now all alone in the cold and dark city, feeling very lost and isolated.

35
Home Calling

Lilly Baccino hummed to herself while she watched the bright blue skies, eagerly looking out for the first birds to return to the garden. It was now mid-March, and for the last few days, the old woman had wrapped up warmly and sat on the canal deck, next to the empty barber's chair, waiting patiently to share her home once again. The aviary in the garden was very quiet. The handful of robins enjoyed the space and calm that winter brought to them.

As she peered at the horizon, Lilly spotted two, then possibly three, specks of fluttering dots in the morning sky. She didn't have to wait long to confirm that it was indeed three familiar sand martins, returning from elsewhere in Europe to enjoy the Baccino garden once again. The sand martins glided above the canal as they rapidly swept up to perch on the overhead branches of the tall apple tree. Lilly smiled as she admired the distinctive dark chest-bar of the new arrivals. The old lady was instantly relieved that she had left some hanging bags of nuts around the garden. It would have been so rude not to have a welcome feast in place.

She looked across at the barber's chair, and although she knew it was empty and that no response would come, she spoke anyway. "You see, Dennis. Life goes on, it never stops. It's the order of the earth. I told you we just had to trust nature!"

Lilly folded her arms and as she smiled to herself, wondering how her Dennis would have reacted, she heard footsteps approaching. She looked up and was warmed by the sight of her beautiful granddaughter, walking towards her with a real sense of purpose. She also noticed the head of UMA, delicately peeking out of the summer house window, his large glowing yellow eyes quickly giving his position away, even though it looked like he was trying to hide from view. It was then that Lilly noticed Velia Rose was carrying a tray with teacups, a plate of biscuits, and a large red teapot. Velia Rose reached her grandmother and rested the tray on the table, and it was then that Mrs Baccino raised her old, cold hand to her chest as she noticed that the red teapot carried several large chips and deep cracks.

The old lady stared at it for a few moments and then looked to Velia Rose to confirm that it was the very same teapot that had broken on the day that Dennis Baccino left them. Without a word being said, Velia Rose had already sensed the question and was nodding with a restrained smile. She moved close to her grandmother and gently pulled her up from the old comfy seat that she had occupied. She gently ushered her over to the old barber's chair as Lilly looked a little bewildered.

"What are you doing, my darling? This is my Dennis's chair. I don't sit here. I don't think I can get up into that thing. Velia Rose, what are you doing, darling?" asked the curious Lilly as she was slowly lifted and eased into the great, comfortable barber's chair. The old lady became even more confused when Velia Rose turned the barber's chair away from the garden so that it now faced the canal. A passing barge gently chugged by, its skipper politely nodding to the little old lady, who looked tiny and baffled as she sat in the large leather chair.

Lilly Baccino was a small woman, and her feet dangled above the old silver footrest. She sat there, not totally sure why Velia Rose had placed her in the old chair. Then she noticed the familiar smell of Dennis Baccino. It was his soapy aftershave smell that she recognised instantly, and it made her flush with joy. It was then that she thought she heard a tiny crackling sound, a background sound that she had heard countless times before. The sound of Italian orchestra strings filled the spring morning air and Lilly could feel the barber's chair begin to slowly turn around, smoothly revolving her to face the garden once more. She was already full of emotion, but she was not at all prepared for what happened next as the barber's chair stopped and she faced Velia Rose and UMA.

She was numb with surprise and awe. A nervous Velia Rose and UMA stood at the edge of the table, and before them sat the old Symphola gramophone, playing her favourite music from its familiar old brass horn. She shook her head in disbelief. It couldn't be. It just couldn't be. It had been completed destroyed!

She stared at the gramophone in amazement, It wasn't just that the old gramophone had been magically restored, for in itself that would be a miracle. She was enchanted and hypnotised by what was etched and painted on the sides of the case. She leant forward with both hands now trembling and her mouth fell open.

The old gramophone case had three panelled cabinet doors. On the cabinet's left door, she could see a perfect drawing of her younger self, the image of a beautiful young bride standing alone. She then glanced at the cabinet's right door and she caught her breath in amazement at the young, handsome figure of Dennis Baccino, standing waiting at an altar, looking exactly like he did on the day they became man and wife. Lilly's body trembled as she moved her view to the middle cabinet. On it danced a young couple. It was a wedding dance, and they looked very much in love.

The music continued to play and Lilly Baccino could no longer contain her emotions. Tears flowed from a soul that brimmed full of happiness and sadness. The old lady opened her arms, and Velia Rose rushed to hold her dear grandmother. UMA stood still, feeling a little inadequate as they embraced, his heart light now shining in a full bright red bloom. UMA even remained still when he felt a gentle hand rest upon his cold metal shoulder.

"*Dio Mio!*" shrieked Lilly as she looked up, still cradling Velia Rose in her arms, the young woman's face buried from view as it was nestled into her grandmother's neck. Velia Rose could feel her grandmother's heartbeat against her own and she turned to see what had shocked her emotional grandmother. As she did, she almost froze and realised that hearts really could miss a beat.

Standing in front of her was Robert Karma, offering a gentle smile that she could never resist. Robert lightly patted UMA on the shoulder as he boldly moved towards Velia Rose, reaching out his warm, steady hand and gently lifting her from Lilly Baccino's arms and sweeping her into his own. He raised a hand to rest on her pale cheek before reaching down to kiss her. It was a kiss that came from deep inside of him, a kiss he had wanted to deliver since he could remember first ever seeing Velia Rose.

Velia Rose held him tight, now dizzy in a dream and lost to the moment. Robert held her tightly as he lifted his head and looked down at UMA, smiling at his old friend as he mouthed a grateful "Thank you". It was nearly the most romantic moment in the history of humanity, but fell slightly short of this when Lilly clumsily knocked and clanked the cracked red teapot against the teacups before exclaiming, "*Bellissimo!* Now, who fancies a nice cuppa?"

***

A few hours passed in the garden and everything felt so comfortable and right again. Of course, nothing would be the same, but it felt like a new beginning that everyone needed. It was now twilight, and Lilly Baccino was at the kitchen window, preparing a homecoming feast and singing as she made a large cheese topped lasagne filled with her secret Italian recipe pasta sauce. The aviary was filling up nicely, which caused a few of the robins to grumble about having to share the bird food in the garden. The fountain waters flowed, and the fisherman statue revolved around the gentle waters, still searching into the evening skies as the small lighthouse that sat on top of the summer house shone its long yellow beam into the coming dark.

UMA diligently watered some promising young flower buds, his old reliable watering can gently soaking the various flowers and plants. The first butterfly of the year rested on the back of the little robot's hand, allowing UMA to study and cherish its beautiful colours. Robert and Velia Rose sat at the edge of the canal and held each other's hand. Robert had explained how he had lost himself, and also described what finally triggered his awakening. Velia Rose could understand everything that Robert had said but chose just to nod and smile in her usual silence as she squeezed his hand tenderly, never wanting them to separate again.

Robert looked up towards his parents house and slowly shook his head, "I went to see my Mum and Dad earlier today. They were busy planning the new house move…said they needed a bigger place for more stuff. They were excited about getting a new place with a triple garage, extra dining rooms and a home cinema."

Velia Rose tenderly squeezed Roberts hand as he continued, "They just seem to buy more and more stuff in the hope that it will somehow make them happy. Dad never stops working to pay for it all, but still they repeat the cycle forever. Buy more. Work more. Buy more. Work more…I don't think they will ever change. I really want them to find real happiness one day, but…" Roberts voice trailed away in silent despair as a new sound began to fill the garden.

It was UMA who began to play the first instrument. He sat at the harp stool and reached for the strings as he played some familiar notes – ones that Velia Rose could instantly recognise, for it was a song that they all had played together many years before. UMA had found a way to reach the furthest harp strings by utilising some tools that he could extend from his metal fingertips. The clever robot continued to play as Robert pulled Velia Rose over to the piano that stood on the veranda of the summer house.

Resting on top of the upright piano was a violin. Robert sat at the piano and instinctively followed the tune that the little robot played, as Velia Rose took the violin and then joined in. Lilly smiled as she listened along while she began to dish the freshly cooked food on to the warm plates, ready to take out into the garden. It had been a truly wonderful day, the type of day that made her understand that life was very precious. Life was a gift, with or without her husband.

The trio played on and smiled at each other, almost breaking out of time as they laughed at the now super-dazzling bright red light that illuminated from UMA. Lilly almost danced down the garden path, carrying two plates of delicious food. She passed the musical trio and was about to reach the garden table when she suddenly stopped, quickly rooted to the spot. She stood as still as a statue, for she did not believe what she was hearing. The stunning voice of an angel now filled the garden, singing above a piano and a harp. The voice was strong yet delicate. The voice came from within the heart of Velia Rose.

Robert and UMA played along as Velia Rose stood tall and proud as she sang out into the night. She had both of her hands on Robert's broad shoulders, holding on to him for strength and belief. The silent angel was silent no more.

Lilly dropped the food on to the floor, both plates smashing as she smiled and gazed lovingly at her granddaughter, who had chosen to hide from life no longer. She went to Velia Rose and joined her as they both sang together. The music played on as they finished singing a verse, allowing Velia Rose to whisper to her grandmother, "It's going to be okay, Granny Lilly. My voice got lost, but I found it again. No more hiding from the world. I promise. I love you so much."

UMA was so happy. Everything had come together, and he cherished the music that they all made that night. He watched as his small metal fingers accurately plucked at the harp strings, and then noticed a subtle flashing green glow that appeared through the harp strings. He moved his head to the other side of the harp and could now see that it was the open laptop that was illuminating the night with its bright display. A sand martin that had just returned to the garden now stood perched on the top of the laptop screen, and UMA looked at the screen display and noticed a familiar map of South East China. The map featured a flashing green dot located in a remote coastal area.

During the many years in the garden, UMA had learned how to feel real human emotions. But now after so many years of searching, once again, he didn't know how to feel.

Epilogue : Eternal Light

(Present day in a South-East China fishing village)

It had been a long and challenging journey, and though it was still dark, UMA was now very close to his destination. The path leading up the hill was littered with pastel pink and white petals that had floated down from the cherry blossom trees. He took care not to walk over any of the fallen petals as he trekked up the steep incline. After many years of daily searching, technology had finally given him the information he had desperately sought. He now hoped to have found the only place he finally needed to get to.

The small robot looked up and could see the rooftop of the small dwelling on the peak of the hill. The house stood alone and perched over a small harbour. It looked unloved and possibly unoccupied. Its wood was rotten, many roof tiles were missing, and in the windows hung rag-like curtains, tattered from the nearby salty sea air and gusty coastal winds.

UMA reached the top of the path and now stood to face the entrance of the house. It looked isolated and forgotten. An old bicycle lay on the floor by the front door, which was dimly lit by a single hanging Chinese lantern. UMA could see that the bicycle wheel chain was rusted and deduced that it had not been used for months, maybe years. Old and idle fishing nets lay sprawled next to it.

He noticed a crack on the windowpane in the front door as he lightly tapped on it, before giving a gentle knock on the tired-looking wooden panel. After a few minutes of no response, he eased the unlocked door open and stepped into the dark, damp hallway. The little robot creaked over an old floorboard, which prompted a weak, limp voice in a nearby room to call out to him.

"Who is it? Is there someone out there?"

UMA moved towards the voice and entered a downstairs room. It was a small, cold, dark bedroom. On the bed in the corner lay a very old man, maybe close to 100 years old, his head straining to lift itself to get a view of his visitor.

"Please, tell me who it is? I live alone and have no money. There is nothing to take."

UMA reached the side of the bed and was only an arm's reach away from the sick old man. The old man continued whispering with his eyes closed. "I am dying, and I do not expect to see the next sunrise. I am beyond any help now."

UMA placed his hand on the arm of the old man. His metallic hand was cold and shining with the dewy condensate of the new day about to begin. The old man was just as cold, and UMA realised his life was close to ending. The old man looked up at the robot, and it took him a few moments to register and recall who was at the side of his bed, and then somehow he seemed to gain strength.

"No Not, you! You are one of the robots from the old factory, I remember, I remember. There were thousands of machines just like you. Damn you! You and those robots replaced all the workers and me. I lost my job. I lost my family and my beautiful son. I lost my life. Curse you! Get out and let me die alone!"

UMA's hand gently squeezed the old man's before it was pushed away.

"Just, please, leave me alone. I have lived here alone, for many years, and I choose to die alone now." The old man was about to close his eyes, as he was weak and tired and a very deep sleep seemed to be calling him. A warm red glow shined on to the old man's wrinkled face, and the old man squinted at the red glowing orb on the robot's chest.

The red light flickered, and a distant shadowy image of a familiar and beautifully pure face appeared within the dim red glow. It was the face of a ten-year-old Chinese boy. It was the young face of Changpu Yamanuchi. The old man's eyes widened as if in disbelief and he thought he must now be passing into the next world and that dreams were now his reality.

A familiar voice came from the face inside the robot. "Father, it is me, your son, Changpu. I have searched for you for so long. I never stopped looking."

"This cannot be!" cried the sick, old man. "I lost my son many years ago." Tears coated his old eyes as he affectionately and instinctively reached out to touch the image of his son's face, which seemed frozen within the robot's heart light. The old man's eyes were now hypnotised by the boy he loved so much.

"I can explain," whispered the young voice.

The old man was still in a state of disbelief. "You must hurry and tell me, for I am dying."

The face of young Changpu nodded from UMA's heart light as he continued. "When I was left all alone, I had nothing. I worked very hard and found success, wealth, and fame, but I did not find love, only loneliness. People thought I had everything, but really, I had nothing. Eventually, my physical body started to fail me, but I would not allow myself to fully pass into the next world until I had experienced real human feelings and true love – and until I found you again.

"After many years of hard work and research, I tried but could not create artificial emotion. But I managed to discover a way to transfer my spirit and soul to this robot. The transfer process returned me to the happiest time of my life, when I was ten years old and went fishing with you every day. I now understand that only humans and living things can ever possess pure emotion. We are unique in our capacity for love. This robot is merely a physical vessel that carries my spirit and soul."

The old man was now transfixed and could only shake his head in puzzled wonderment.

Changpu's voice went on. "Being inside this robot has gifted me more time, for that is what we only have in this life. For the last six years, my feelings and emotions have lived through this robot, and my life has been truly extraordinary."

The old man made a great effort to slowly raise his head, half amazed, but also very ill and weak. "What did you see, my son? Tell me, be quick!"

"I experienced the wonderful gift of real and loving friendships. I witnessed a new young love blossom, and also how old love endures and still grows, even after many years, even after loss. I learned about strength and hope. I can see how man can be easily blinded by greed and lose touch with what really matters in life. Many people get lost in modern life. They search for meaning and happiness in things that cannot return any love. Most people are too busy or distracted, even to ever wonder if they are truly happy. They forget about love . . . the one special thing that makes them truly human."

His father slowly nodded. "It seems you have learned much and understand life, my son. I am so sorry that it's too late to find love again with me. As much as I have missed you dearly, I am about to leave this world."

The robot's head nodded, as he then looked around the sparse and dank bedroom. Under a small bedside table was an old bamboo box, filled with many old photos and newspaper cuttings of how Changpu Yamanuchi had become the wealthiest man in the world.

"I was very proud of you, my son, but I let my pride and ego rule my heart. I came here many years ago to be alone and to escape the pain of losing you. Many times I tried to reach you at the robotics company, but they always turned me away because I was an old and poor fisherman. No one would believe that I was the father of the richest man in the world. They said I was just another beggar."

This time, the old man reached for the robot's hand as his old eyes remained lovingly locked on the young boy's face, which was still illuminated from the red haze.

"Now it's my time to go, Changpu, but I am so relieved and happy to tell you that I never stopped loving you, my son."

The young boy's fuzzy, pixelated face smiled as he whispered to the dying man, "Father, I never stopped loving you either. There is another way. I came here to save you."

The old man did not understand and was now fading fast. He slowly rocked his head and gazed up at the old shabby wall next to his bed, staring at an old wooden photo frame hanging on a rusted nail. It was a picture that he looked at every single day. It somehow lifted his spirits whenever he felt lonely. It was an old black-and-white photo, yellowed at the edges, of a smiling father and his son proudly displaying the catch of the day on the sands of the old fishing harbour. Whenever he looked at that photo, he would close his eyes and could easily return to that moment in time. It was his most treasured memory. He closed his eyes, hoping to go back to that place in time just once more again.

Just then, another robot then entered the room and stood next to UMA, at the side of the old man's bed. The robot was almost identical to UMA but did not have the inscribed letters that Robert and Velia Rose had scribed on to UMA's chest to make it read "hUMAn". It carried the serial number 002 from 002 on the manufacturer's plate attached to the back of its round metal head.

The old man stirred again and looked momentarily confused but then beamed one last time at the face of Changpu, illuminated in UMA's heart light, before he took his final breath. In that very same moment, UMA took the old man's hand and placed it on the circular glass panel of the other robot. A stark white searing light shone from the other robot as the frail human hand made contact with the circular glass panel. The light grew more intensive as a groaning deep throbbing sound shook the walls of the old house.

Suddenly the light faded, and the only sound within the hilltop house was a slowly fading humming sound. The body of the old man in the bed was now still and lifeless. His cold face looked now at peace as the first sounds of birdsong arrived to meet the new day.

The two robots slowly turned to face each other as UMA placed his hand on the other robot's shoulder. Both of the robots' heart lights now pulsed and beat together in concert, like two shimmering red spheres. The young face of Changpu Yamanuchi still peered out from UMA's glowing heart light, and his face smiled as the familiar face of his father surfaced in the heart glow of the other robot.

It was not the very old face that belonged to the dead man on the bed, but the handsome face of his thirty-year-old father – the proud man who would happily take him fishing every day. The two bright faces smiled at each other, as the voice of Changpu's father broke the silence.

"Can we ever go fishing again my, son?" he asked with hopeful eyes and a trembling, nervous voice.

The face of Changpu filled with joy. The young boy gratefully nodded within the red haze as he replied happily, "Oh Father, at last you see, that is all I have ever wanted."

***

The old woman sat by the old harbour, watching all the local fishermen push away in their small boats, all of them hoping for fair weather and a good catch. It was first light, and a new day was beginning as she noticed two unusual figures walking down the hill and along the beach, fishing nets draped around their shoulders. As they neared her, one of the strange figures paused and gently waved to the old woman. She didn't quite understand why, but she instinctively returned a hopeful smile and an eager wave.

They dragged a small fishing boat from the dry morning sands and pushed it out into the shallow waves as they jumped aboard, both glowing in excited anticipation of a new day. *They seem like two happy souls*, the old woman thought. She watched as they drifted away from land and glided out to meet the early morning horizon. She stared at the silhouetted image of a father and son, happily fishing together under a deep eternal sun.

The old woman nodded to herself and smiled, her distant memory recalling how she had watched them take to the sea when she was a young girl, almost a lifetime ago. The angelic rising red sun was perfectly reflected on the calm, deep blue tides.

The majestic horizon now flourished as it revealed two shimmering red spheres.

End

I do hope you enjoyed The Loneliest Robot!
Before you go, I would like to request a big favour that would be a
big help to a new author.

Could you *please* leave a reader review on Amazon?
It would be greatly appreciated!

Authors Note

This book is about getting lost in modern life.

Its very easy to get lost in our busy and fast-moving times. We can lose ourselves in so many things…technology, career, over consumption, television, money, etc.

Some people lose themselves and forget who they really are, while some people get lost through circumstance and poor fortune.

Material things, work obsession and being immersed in technology - these things cannot return love, but can certainly absorb all our time, energy and attention.

Try not to lose yourself chasing all that stuff - it's a distraction to finding true happiness.
*Take time to enjoy and value **people** and our wonderful **planet**.*

It may not always be the easy thing, but choose life!
Your heart and loved ones will thank you for it.

Andrew Glennon

About the Author

The Loneliest Robot is the debut novel from Andrew Glennon.

Andrew is based in England and is a husband and
proud father of twins.

A Business Graduate and Commercial Real Estate professional, he has
over 25 years experience of working in many parts of the world for large
global companies.

He walked away from all of that stuff because it didn't
make him happy.

Andrew likes having fun with his family and enjoys meeting
interesting people, music, concerts and great movies. He is getting slightly
better at golf.

Andrew dislikes robotic greedy people, mindless TV, advertising,
margarine and rap music.

Visit the author's website at;
www.theloneliestrobot.com

Contact the author at;
andrew_glennon@yahoo.com

Made in the USA
Middletown, DE
30 July 2017